The Author

GABRIELLE ROY was born in St. Boniface, Manitoba, in 1909. Her parents were part of the large Quebec emigration to western Canada in the late nineteenth century. The youngest of eight children, she studied in a convent school for twelve years, then taught school herself, first in isolated Manitoba villages and later in St. Boniface.

In 1937 Roy travelled to Europe to study drama, and during two years spent in London and Paris she began her writing career. The approaching war forced her to return to Canada, and she settled in Montreal.

Roy's first novel, *The Tin Flute*, ushered in a new era of realism in Quebec fiction with its compassionate depiction of a working-class family in Montreal's Saint-Henri district. Her later fiction often turned for its inspiration to the Manitoba of her childhood and her teaching career.

In 1947 Roy married Dr. Marcel Carbotte, and after a few years in France, they settled in Quebec City, which was to remain their home. Roy complemented her fiction with essays, reflective recollections, and three children's books. Her many honours include three Governor General's Awards, France's Prix Fémina, and Quebec's Prix David.

Gabrielle Roy died in Quebec City, Quebec, in 1983.

GABRIELLE ROY

Garden in the Wind

Translated by Alan Brown

With an Afterword by Dennis Cooley

M&S

Un jardin au bout du monde
Original Edition
Copyright © 1975 Gabrielle Roy
Garden in the Wind
Translated by Alan Brown
Copyright © 1977 by McClelland and Stewart Limited
Afterword copyright © 1989 by Dennis Cooley
New Canadian Library edition 1989

Canadian Cataloguing in Publication Data

Roy, Gabrielle, 1909-1983
[Un jardin au bout du monde. English]
Garden in the Wind

(New Canadian library)
Translation of: Un jardin au bout du monde.
Bibliography: p.
ISBN 0-7710-9857-X

I. Title   II. Title: Un jardin au bout du monde. English.   III. Series.

PS8535.O95J3713 1989   C843´.54   C89-094471-7
PQ3919.R74J3713 1989

We acknowledge the financial support of the Government of
Canada through the Book Publishing Industry Development Program
for our publishing activities. We further acknowledge the support of the
Canada Council for the Arts and the Ontario Arts Council for our
publishing program.

Printed and bound in Canada

McClelland & Stewart Inc.
The Canadian Publishers
481 University Avenue
Toronto, Ontario
M5G 2E9

2 3 4 5   03 02 01 00 99

Garden in the Wind

Contents

_F_ar be it from me to propose an interpretation of my writings or characters to those kind enough to be my readers. I would much prefer to know what they think about these things.

For once, however, I think it may be useful to give some explanation of the short stories in this book. Two of them, published elsewhere, appear here in reworked form. The first, _A Tramp at the Door_, was rewritten more than twenty years after its first version. It is a dangerous undertaking to try to tighten the meaning of an old text without losing the candour or the original lyricism that gave birth to it. If I persisted in taking up this story again it is because it represents rather well, I think, the slightly medieval or "holy-image" aspect under which, far out on the plains, when I was a child, Quebec appeared to us, through the medium of our parents' stories on the subject. They were immigrants to Manitoba, but they had never, in their hearts, left their Lower Canada behind, and they embroidered, they embroidered. . . . If ever Quebec held an irresistible attraction for its scattered children

9

it was surely at that time, through the magic of tales told around the old Majestic stove.

More or less for the same reason I dug out again the story *Hoodoo Valley*, a fairly just account, I thought, of the chimerical dreams that guided so many immigrants of Eastern and Central Europe in their settlement in the lands of the Canadian West: poor people who, because they had tried to follow their star, ended in the most total disillusionment. These unlucky dreams I learned of through the recollections of my father who, as an officer of the federal government, had the responsibility for settling many colonies of Slavic origin, and particularly a group of Doukhobors, "people as gentle," he said, "as they were impossible to convince."

The two other stories in this volume were not previously published. *Where Will You Go, Sam Lee Wong?* was left for a long time at the stage of a first sketch, abandoned, as it were, along the road, and would no doubt have stayed there had it not been for the persistent way in which this Chinese came back to haunt me, reminding me that I might be the only one who had imagined his life and, as a result, was able to give it reality. What power such a summons has over a writer's heart, coming out of God knows what limbo from a character begging to be given life!

In the same way, *Garden in the Wind* was born of the passing vision I had one day of a garden filled with flowers at the very outer limit of cultivated territory, and of a woman working there, in the wind, a kerchief on her head, who looked up and followed me with a long, perplexed and supplicating gaze which never left my memory and never ceased to demand – for years and years – the thing we are all asking for, from the very depths of our silence: Tell about my life.

G.R.

A Tramp at the Door

A Tramp at the Door

My mother was expecting something or other. She kept going to the door, drawing back from the windowpane the white curtain hemmed in red linen and staring long and vaguely out at the drenched countryside. Suddenly she gave a start, one hand going up to her forehead.

"Somebody's coming," she announced, and went on, her voice filled with surprise: "Coming here, it looks like!"

Rain was rattling on the roof. On either side of the house we could hear water from the spouts splashing down from the overflowing rain barrels. Evening was falling. From the ditches, filled to their banks, a white steam went up. Beyond the slope of the rye field you could see no more than a few blackened, bare treetops emerging soaked from the mist. For two days we hadn't seen a living soul pass by. "Not a cat, not even a beggar," my mother had sighed.

The man pushed the gate open. We could see him tip back his head and try to smile as he saw the two gable windows of the house and perhaps the smoke from the chimney. With every step he had to fight the wind, pulling his dark coat tight around him. The garden shrubs near him were twisted and tousled by the wind. Because of the shadow that already lay dark beneath the hedge, the man was on top of Farouche's kennel before he saw our German shepherd about to spring.

My mother stifled a cry.

Almost at once we saw Farouche wagging his tail, wiggling his body and crouching in front of this man whose strangely gentle, coaxing tone we in the house could catch between the gusts of the storm.

My mother breathed a great sigh, even more astonished than she was relieved.

"Well," she said, "that's the first time I ever saw Farouche make friends that fast!"

The man straightened up and seemed to be surveying all the ways of entering the house. Finally, overcoming his hesitation, he made a half-turn and came rapping on the back door which looked out on the farmyard.

My father, sitting by the fire, was in the grip of the unbearable boredom he suffered with each return of the wet season to our country of the plains. The whole day long he hadn't said a word. You wondered if he really felt he belonged there with the rest of us. Buried in his thoughts, he hadn't seen the stranger coming, and even the sound of our voices had most likely not come through to him.

"It's somebody who doesn't know his way around here." This was my mother again as she gestured to me to open the door.

As soon as autumn came we lived in the big room. The small lean-to that served as a kitchen in the summertime now turned into a kind of storage space where we could pile furniture and tools no longer needed. I went through this freezing space and with difficulty lifted the rusty latch. A wallop of rain took me in the face. The man's head appeared, feebly lit by a vestige of light coming from the big puddles around the

14

pump. All in all, it was a rather nice tramp's face, the kind that isn't any particular age and asks for a bowl of soup and will go on his way right afterwards if he isn't offered an attic for the night. We didn't see those people often in our out-of-the-way parts, maybe one or two a year, if that. But this one seemed to have a certain dignity and wasn't in a hurry to beg. A short, reddish, frizzy beard, pearled with great raindrops, invaded half his cheeks; the peak of his cap threw a clean line of shadow on his forehead. His eyes, very gentle and smiling, almost tender, sparkled under the wet fringe of his lashes.

"Well! My little cousin!" he cried in a voice that was as soft and flexible and unsettling as his gaze. "You must be my little cousin Alice!" he went on, laughing.

I shook my head.

"No? Must be Agnes, then!"

"No," I said, irritated. "I'm Ghislaine."

"Of course, just what I thought! Of course you're Ghislaine. I should have known it, even if I never saw you."

As he spoke, his hands made as if they were drying each other, and he laughed behind his beard and his foot cleverly pushed at the door I was holding slightly open.

Somehow he was inside.

"This is the Rondeaus' house, I guess?" he asked, and his incredible, friendly smile swept around the interior of the damp, cold shed as if he found it welcoming and filled with people.

"No," I said, "we're the Trudeaus."

"Why, sure, just as I was going to say," he went on coolly. "Rondeau, Trudeau, names as like as peas. Right, cousin?"

He gave me a little nudge, and I saw his eyes shining with satisfaction.

"Now, little girl, you just go and tell your father there's a cousin here from the land of Quebec."

I went before him into the big room – he was right on my heels – and blurted out to my father, as if in mocking reproach: "He says he's a cousin from Quebec."

My father stood up and made an odd gesture, as if to take the stranger in his arms, but the impulse failed him. Yet his handsome, aging, peaceful face betrayed not so much a withdrawal as the vagueness of someone suddenly awakened from a dream.

"Well, now! What part of Quebec? Saint-Alphonse?"

"Saint-Alphonse," said the man.

He approached the stove. His clothes were starting to steam. My mother brought the Aladdin lamp. She lifted it a little above the stranger and you could see great rips in his clothing, some held together by bits of string, others gaping to reveal glimpses of his red shirt.

But the man directed at my mother a gaze so filled with friendship that she set down the lamp and busied herself elsewhere without speaking. We could see that she was excited from the way she opened all the drawers of the sideboard without finding what she wanted.

For a moment the man stood alone in the middle of the room, trying to catch our eyes, which fled his. He drew up a chair by the stove, sat down and breathed a great sigh of well-being.

Then in the silence, two or three times, we could hear his soft, rather drawling voice: "Saint-Alphonse, yes sir. That's where I come from. Saint-Alphonse. . . ."

My father took out his tobacco pouch. He was about to fill his pipe when the stranger held out a hand and, unabashed, helped himself to the tobacco. Then, after lighting a short clay pipe, he settled back in his chair and murmured distinctly: "Thank you. Much obliged."

The two men smoked. My mother fussed among her pots

16

with an unusual amount of noise. And sometimes her lips opened as if she were about to say some wounding word. The stranger looked around at us children sitting in the corners, observing one after the other, and smiled out of his beard. He made little jabs with his chin, winked at each of us, then started the rounds again. A badger that we had tamed, still highly suspicious of strangers, actually slipped under the man's chair. He took it by the scruff of its neck and laid it in his lap. The little animal, far from protesting, licked his wet beard and, its claws retracted, allowed itself to be rocked like a baby. As wild and speechless as our only friends – our animals – we were astounded to see that two of them had taken up with this stranger. Even my mother seemed impressed, and that must have aggravated her ill humour. Little by little we slid off our chairs to come nearer. The strange man gave us signs of encouragement in the manner of the magician our parents had once taken us to see at the rodeo in the next village.

My father had stood up. He was pacing to and fro in the room, his hands behind his back. Then, planting himself in front of the vagabond, he asked: "But whose boy would you be then?"

"Me?" said the man. "Why, the one that disappeared."

A glimmer of interest showed beneath my father's lowered eyelids.

"Gustave?"

"Yep. Gustave."

"But they thought he was dead!"

"He wasn't dead. He went to the States. I'm his boy."

"Oh!" said my father. "You're his boy!"

"I'm his boy," the stranger repeated in a voice that was soft and stubborn.

And he turned his smiling face to where my mother was

beating her pancake batter. He seemed determined to drag from her a look, a smile, a word. But she was speeding up her supper preparations so as to stay out of the conversation. It wasn't long before the first spoonful of batter dropped into the hot frying pan. A pleasant odour filled the room. Outside, darkness spread over the desolate, naked landscape. All that could still be seen through the windowpanes was the vague glimmer of water accumulated in great pools between the patches of brush, in the hollows of the plain or running in streams. The man stretched out his legs. He took time to look around the room, low-ceilinged, large, furnished with an oak sideboard and old, modest but solid pieces so well-polished and softened by use that they reflected a long contentment. Then, without moving, he began smiling at nothing again, to himself.

"But what put you onto our trail?" my father asked suddenly.

The stranger raised his blue eyes, which shone in the direct rays of the lamp.

"In Saint-Alphonse."

"Oh!"

My father gave a long sigh.

"It's been a mighty long time since I saw hide or hair of any of them from Saint-Alphonse."

It was his turn to look toward my mother, so tiny, so much younger than he. A big apron tied around her waist, she was leaning attentively above her pan and the flame at times leapt perilously close to her face.

"How long is it now, Albertine, since I was in those parts?"

And indeed it was she who was charged with refreshing his memory on events he had described to her about people she had never seen.

She took a little while to reflect, mentally juggling dates, her pretty eyebrows arched high and her mouth a little open.

"You told me you were fourteen when you left home and you hadn't set foot there since. You figure it out. About fifty years, if you were telling the truth."

She always ended up with that reservation, as if to throw back the error, if error there was, solely upon my father.

Then, sulking a little, and because the stranger's presence doubtless irritated her, she added: "What's more, you haven't written the folks at home for fifteen years. It's a real shame!"

"Yes," said my father, ignoring his wife's last remark. "It'll be fifty years. I wouldn't even know them back there anymore."

He looked down, his face lit up by distant, melancholy memories.

My mother placed her fists on her hips. Quickly, without looking at the stranger, she said: "It's ready! Come on, children. Come and eat, Arthur."

The tramp too stood up gaily. He chose a seat by the wall, slid in, pulling his wretched jacket tight around him, and, once established, seized his fork.

"Yes," my father mused, "there's a lot of things back there I never heard a word about."

The man speared a large slice of bread with his fork. He bit the bread in the middle, then, smiling, his mouth full, he promised: "I'll tell you all about it after."

II

After supper he actually did begin to tell us about the relatives, helped along by my father who would situate things in time by his questions: "Marcelline, now, you must have found she'd aged? And I suppose Eustache took over the farm. . . ."

We knew very little about my father's people. He'd never told us at one time how many brothers and sisters he had. On occasion, and as his reveries would have it, he would let a name drop: Marcelline, Philomène, Aristide. His tone changed, too, according to his mood.

One day, for example, when the soup was too salty, he had grumbled: "Albertine, are you going to start making salty soup like Philomène?"

"Who is Philomène?" we asked.

My father seemed more disconcerted at having provoked the question than by our breathless curiosity. Philomène, he finally admitted, was his father's second wife. A sign from my mother at that moment advised us not to push our researches any further. So it was that my father managed to keep the shades of his childhood for himself alone. At times, though, he himself renewed this singular aura of mystery attached to our uncles and aunts in Quebec. He spoke of ill-defined figures and always in the past tense, as if they had ceased to exist. That's why we were surprised that evening to hear him say, "Marcelline, now, she must have aged?"

Marcelline had made her entry into our family one evening when my father, seeing my mother patching old clothes, protested: "Now don't you start going on like that penny-pincher Marcelline!" The moment his sister's name had slipped out he walled himself in silence.

Others popped up, as faceless as Marcelline. They seemed incredibly far away yet, like that Marcelline, they would suddenly become attached to our lives through their penchant for patching old rags or because of a dreamy warmth that would spread at twilight through the house. And we never knew how many shadowy beings would rise up at our next question, behind Philomène or Marcelline, or if they'd be revealed thanks to some irritation of my father's or in a moment of more tender feeling. One thing we did know: you had to wait for these confidences, never push.

Well, that evening my father sat close to our strange visitor and, behold, names were flying from his lips, those associated with his ill humour as well as the ones we heard on feast days – and others we had never heard at all: Uncle France, Aunt Eléonore, Cousin Brault. You'd have thought a dike that had stood too long against the past had given under the flood of hurrying memories. The visitor gave little signs of approval. His eyes followed my father with an attentiveness that was ingratiating, sustained and encouraging, an attentiveness I have in later life observed in very few human beings. Truly, we might have imagined that it was my father who had just arrived from his travels and that the other one was there only to corroborate the facts or testify to them.

At last, when my father gave the other his turn, our visitor started in with his own stories. He spoke in a restful voice that he seldom raised. He dipped into his memories as into a heap of thick and rustling leaves, fallen at the trees' roots, in autumn.

We, the Trudeaus, were, according to him, a family out of the ordinary. The old couple, alas! had died working, on land that was richer in stones than pasture. But they had left behind them solid testimonials to their ingenuity, a thousand things well done, well carried out, if it was no more than a fence, a barn door or a delicately sculptured weathercock on the roof of that same barn. Whereas nowadays. . . .

Several times he stopped to make sure that my father was listening with pleasure. In fact, my father seemed to have changed, to have emerged from a kind of penumbra as he renewed touch, so to speak, with his family, divided and scattered to all corners of the country by obscure misfortunes or obstinacies. In one swift glance our visitor would seize the trace of an emotion; then, sure of his trail, he would take off again without more emphasis but as if animated by a great desire to please.

What began to strike us then about this singular creature was that from the depths of his solitude he accused no one but seemed rather to assume all faults himself.

On the subject of family, however, it can't be said that he gave us many important details that first evening. Apart from that, he described minutely Christmas parties, New Years' parties, winter-evening parties, wedding parties, and suddenly Montreal, the great city, and suddenly Joliette, the small city, where the people of Saint-Alphonse went shopping. Then he'd comment on pioneer days, only to drift unexpectedly to meals of buckwheat cakes and wild honey or memories of square dances in the kitchen; and we'd see my

22

father tapping lightly on the floor with toe and heel.

But already, through our visitor's account, these vague, far-off relatives of ours all seemed to have changed their characters – even Marcelline, who was no longer grasping, only provident. Eustache had inherited the paternal land and made it bear fruit; he raised his children courageously. Anais, now, there was nobody like her for spinning the local wool and filling the cupboard with bolts of homespun. Devout she was, too, never missed her week-day mass. Uncle France had made it to a hundred, and they'd had a fine Christian birthday for him with all the children and grandchildren, of whom two were attending the seminary and three had taken vows. Family was something sacred: nothing could be as touching as the members of a single family knowing each other by their voices and opening their arms. Alas, people sometimes rejected their own flesh and blood when it turned up from afar, especially if it wasn't very clean or a particularly shining case.

This was said in a tone of resignation that made us all hang our heads, except my mother who, on the contrary, raised hers defiantly. She was sewing, a little off to one side, sticking her needle so impatiently into the cloth that she often pricked herself. Then we could hear her groan softly as she put her lips to the finger where a drop of blood was forming.

In the middle of a silence my father asked: "Marcelline, now . . . did she ever mention me, sometimes?"

The man assured him warmly: "Oh, for sure! She often talked about her brother. . ."

"Arthur." My father completed the sentence.

"That's it, Arthur."

My father pulled up his chair until his foot almost touched the stranger's muddy boots. He lit his pipe for the fourth time and asked a question that astonished us greatly.

23

"Did they know back there that I'd been appointed justice of the peace?"

"They knew it," affirmed the vagabond. "Marcelline was very proud."

A happy silence followed, broken by my mother's noisy sigh.

The man turned in her direction: "What about you, cousin, which parish are you from? Maybe I know your people too. . . ."

My mother rose up, all round and little and trembling at this mode of address, as if the stranger's hand had touched her.

"She's from the prairies," my father hastened to explain. "I married her out here."

"What of it?" the man insisted. "I've drifted around every which way at harvest times. Maybe I knew her folks."

No one took him up on it. The man seemed hurt. A little later his pale-blue gaze grew fixed and we could see that he was close to sleep. For a second his eyelids would drop, his eyes would glaze, and before they closed you could see in them a vague smile of apology and a slightly crestfallen expression.

It had just struck eleven. But my mother was acting as if the evening had just begun. My father, for his part, kept looking at the clock, pulling out his watch and comparing the two. The stranger dozed in his chair for minutes at a time, then awoke with a start, trying to cover up by winking at each of us in turn and changing posture.

My father said suddenly: "Hey, children! It's bedtime!" Then, without waiting for my mother's approval, he suggested: "Maybe you could make up a bed, Albertine. . ." He hesitated, then concluded: ". . .for our cousin. . . ."

"Gustave. After my father," explained the stranger,

yawning. "Gustave, that's me."

My mother stood up without a word, took the lamp and left us in shadows and then in darkness as she went up the steps leading to the attic. We could hear her moving a cot around, opening trunks. Through the half-open trap door a cold draught swept down on our shoulders, soon bearing with it the odour of fresh linen.

Later, having awakened, I could hear my mother speaking in a low voice to my father: "You always told me your brother Gustave was built like a giant, tall and broad, the strongest one in the family. This one's a puny runt. . . ."

"Far as that goes," my father replied, "you take any family around here. The big men don't always have the big sons. Maybe he takes after his mother," he added after a pause.

"That may be, but couldn't you see he was at a loss for an answer when you asked him for news of Marcelline and Philomène? "

"That's only natural. He's been on the road a lot. It couldn't all come back at once."

"Oh, that's the excuse, is it?" exclaimed my mother in a hostile, discouraged tone.

In the next room to theirs the man was snoring peacefully. Once he mumbled a few words in his sleep. Then I thought I heard, at the end of a jovial little laugh: "Good day! Good day, dear cousin!"

III

He stayed at our house three weeks. My mother gave him some clothes left by a former hired man, and they were about Gustave's size. Early in the morning, he used to wash in the kitchen sink, and comb his beard, and turn out quite presentable.

During the day he tried to make himself useful and took special pains to anticipate my mother's wishes. He'd bring in wood; run to the well as soon as the pail was dry, repair the traps. One day when she complained there'd been no mail for a week because of the roads, he went off on foot to the village. He came back at day's end with a letter which he held out to her in the hope, no doubt, of getting a friendly word.

In spite of everything we couldn't get used to the idea that he was supposed to be our cousin. We ordered him around like a farm hand. "Better get the wood in before the rain soaks it." In the daytime we called him "you" or "the man" or "him." My mother, above all, because she was afraid of having him with us all winter, would say each morning, looking out at the road unwinding toward the dark, dank woods:

"There's going to be a big snowstorm before long. A person won't even be able to get out of here."

The man seemed not to hear. In the daytime we paid little attention to him. But in the evening, as soon as the lighted lamp stood on the table, this strange creature, through what kind of spell we didn't know, became indispensable to us. Every evening he again turned into "Cousin Gustave."

He appeared sensitive to this kind of disgrace, of which we absolved him every evening. Silent the whole day long, he regained the use of words as soon as our eyes, grown softer, consented to look at him again. Then, in his quiet, unchanging voice, he would once more tell the story of Marcelline's second wedding, or Uncle France's hundredth birthday, but always adding fresh details. "Hey, you didn't mention that last time!" my father would cry. And Gustave would look at him with a vague reproach in his eyes, as if he wanted to say: The things I know are too vast, too many-sided. You can't get all that out at once.

"Well, go on," my father would hurry him.

Gustave, cut adrift from his vision, would set off again, but on a new tack.

His stories proceeded by short stages, often interrupted at the most touching or fascinating part, so that we were always inclined to give him another day of hospitality in order to hear the end. And finally we had to admit it to ourselves: if Gustave's story the previous night had been a good one, we were polite and well disposed toward him the following day. But when he'd disappointed us, we had ways, unconsciously but cruelly, of showing him.

Well, this fellow Gustave grew very skilful. He spun his stories out. He cut them into little slices in a way that later became familiar to us through the radio. Everything was used to stretch them out. The landscape would be painstakingly described. The village teacher, the notary and the doctor had their parts to play. Jumping from one family to the next, it might happen that he got into events that barely concerned us but livened up his story immeasurably. There was one about the son of Magloire the blacksmith who hanged himself in the barn with his own belt; and the one about Fortunat who, at the age of twenty, married a rich widow of fifty.

One evening, when I pointed out that all this had nothing to do with us, he turned toward me a look that was courageous and untamed: "Come now! Who's related to who? There's a question: where it starts, where it stops, who knows?"

Then, as if he realized that our suspicions could be nourished by this odd remark, he gave a little strangled laugh and went patiently back to the tale that especially pleased my father, about Marcelline's second wedding. Little by little he grew lively again, and treated us to the fiddler who had made Marcelline, at fifty-five, dance for the first time in her life.

"What! She got up and danced?" asked my father.

"Yes, sir, she danced!" Gustave affirmed.

And in his eyes as pale as water we thought we saw Marcelline's cotton lustre skirt whirl and pass by.

"So she got up and danced!" repeated my father, delighted.

One night my father mentioned two of his brothers who had also settled out West, Uncle Alfred in Saskatchewan and Uncle Edouard in Alberta. In a sentimental mood, he admitted his regret that he had failed to keep in touch at least with these two.

Gustave let my father go on for some time, then he promised, in that spell-binding voice which sometimes sang through our house like the winds of the wide world: "Who knows, maybe I'll drop in and see them one of these days! You just give me the right address and if the good Lord wills, I'll give them your regards."

That was all that was said about our western uncles, whom we had seen only once, Alfred when he had started off from Montreal and stopped to see us on the way, and Edouard when he had arrived from Quebec with his family and almost settled nearby.

As Gustave could give us no news of these two, my father asked for more news from Quebec, in particular about a charlatan he had known in his youth and who, it seemed, had made a fortune.

"Oh, yes! Ephrem Brabant!" said Gustave.

And that evening he began a story that lasted almost a week.

This charlatan, Ephrem Brabant by name, had started off by handing out samples of his cough syrup to the congregation as they left the chilly church on Sunday mornings. But the remedy that someone had taken for his cold had miraculously cured him of another much more serious illness. Thanks to an early spring, the news of the cure spread rapidly around the countryside. It was at once attributed to Ephrem, who was a "seventh son."

Now Ephrem wasn't about to belittle the powers and properties of his remedy any more than he denied the supernatural gifts attributed to him. A pious man, gentle and charitable, he was quite ready to admit that faith helped medicine along. So, as he enjoined his customers to prayer, he sold them more and more little bottles. The same herbal product with different labels and in different containers brought relief to stomach cramps, asthma and rheumatic pains.

Ephrem's renown spread beyond the limits of the village. Soon he had a little covered cart and a horse as black as night, and he went from farm to farm leaving brown bottles wherever he stopped. People in perfect health tried his remedy and declared they felt none the worse, which added to Ephrem Brabant's prestige as much as the cures themselves. He had grown a beard, which he trimmed to a point, and wore a black, wide-rimmed hat. His photo appeared on the bottles of syrup. Everyone in the area called him Dr. Brabant. It was at this time that he had the notion of writing and distributing an almanac to publicize the testimonials of people cured by his attentions. It was to contain, as well, practical advice for people of various ages, the interpretation of dreams and all the known signs of good or inclement weather. The fellow could neither read nor write, but he had immense practical knowledge based on direct observation of rural life. For the spelling and fine phrases he depended on a son he had sent to school. He moved to Montreal, to a luxurious house, and despite being hauled to court, he accumulated a tidy fortune.

This was the story Gustave told us. Or, rather, this was the version we created with the passage of time and according to our desire to draw our own conclusions. Gustave must have told it more simply, and perhaps with more indulgence. For he blamed no one, judged no one. Almost every creature found mercy before him. If some really bad ones turned up, Gustave had them die off quickly, which in the end appeased my mother.

IV

Now that I think of it, it's true he talked very little about the members of our own family, apart from saying they were fine people. The unforgettable ones he managed to dig up elsewhere. After the story of Brabant, he told us about Roma Poirier who murdered her husband by putting ground glass in his soup day after day. Oh, the strange, cruel and fascinating beings he brought to our place in the evenings, when the pails swung and rattled on the fence posts outside and from the woodland's edge coyotes yapped incessantly.

Long after he had left, as unexpectedly as he had come, long after his features had blurred in our memories, or his gentle way of smiling as he talked of the most sinister events, it would happen that those characters – the charlatan, the murderess, the old man of a hundred and I don't know how many more – would turn up in our thoughts. A whole unconnected cohort, the friends of Gustave the tramp, who revealed them to us perhaps less through his words than through a certain slow way of pulling back his coat as he reflected on their lives, or by an occasional amused smile at the troop of them.

He knew the great wickedness of the world quite well but he neither judged it nor renounced it. Nor the great distress of the world. Of that he sometimes gave us a glimpse beneath his heavy eyelids, as he stared at a windowpane whipped by rain and branches.

But, above all, it was the great piety of the world that he had seen and recognized.

And through this, in the end, he found grace even in my mother's eyes.

One night he was telling about the pilgrims flocking to the sanctuary of Sainte-Anne-de-Beaupré. The nave appeared before us, filled with votive offerings, with longboats and schooners for lamps. Thousands of crutches hung between the stations of the Cross, as if the lame, on their march toward God, had recovered their agility and taken off for heaven through the pale openings of the stained-glass windows. A pious murmur rose in the shadows; our house was too small to contain the piety of the pilgrims, their thanksgiving, their wild hope. Gustave led us beyond all the paths we knew. We followed his blue gaze, a pool of water in the night, toward a dim region through which he led us to the sound of chants and organs.

There was always someone who sighed loudly when Gustave's voice fell silent and we came back to the reality of our house.

Of course he mixed up times and persons, but which of us, living on the prairie, far from the beaten path, could have told true from false in his accounts?

He had quickly seen that the mistress of the house appeared to listen only when he talked of miracles and pilgrimages. From that moment we could get him to speak of nothing else. He carried us to the places of prayer up and down the length of the St. Lawrence. At the very words "St. Lawrence," we were captured at once, for he had given us such a gripping vision of the river. He talked of it as a living creature, a tumultuous force, and yet at times so kind that its flow made no more than a murmur. He had described it as having its source in the Niagara cataracts (he was a little careless about geographical accuracy). Then he showed us how it fled toward the sea, encircling a great island whose name we loved: Anticosti.

Then one evening he ran out of places of prayer on the St. Lawrence. And he began to describe St. Joseph's Oratory, built stone after stone with the people's offerings. My mother (she had a special devotion for Brother André) stopped sewing and for the first time spoke directly to Gustave. She normally addressed him through the mediation of one of the children. "Ask him," she'd say, "if he's seen the hammer"; or, "Was he the one that took the shovel? See if you can find out. . . ." For in the process of making himself useful he mislaid things, and my mother, who would have had scruples about accusing him directly, didn't hesitate to burden him with a latent guilt.

But this time she looked him in the eye and said: "Tell me, did you ever see him? Brother André?"

Perhaps Gustave felt the full risk of a careless answer. My mother, depending on her mood, would give him a heaping plateful at dinner, or nothing but the less tasty scraps. Did he understand the thirst for spiritual adventure that lived in this serious little woman, sentimental and deprived of the joys of church? Could he conceive of her longing for "back home," she who had been born out here in the plains? And maybe, after all, he *had* seen Brother André, for had he not assured us that he'd seen the Prince of Wales and Sarah Bernhardt? In any case, he described him to us so faithfully that much later, when we received a calendar from Quebec bearing a lithograph of the saintly Brother, we all exclaimed, "That was him, sure enough!"

For greater effect he assured us at the end, after his accumulation of evidence: "I saw him the way I see you now...Madame!"

He no longer dared to say "Cousin" to her, but could not pronounce "Madame" without a perceptible hesitation and a note of regret.

From that moment on he grew in my mother's esteem. Henceforth, she gave him an attention which if not always benevolent was at least sustained.

V

But this state of affairs didn't last long. This little devil of
a man, who could down plates of porridge in the early morning and fried pork piled up on his plate at other meals without
putting on a pound, this "puny runt," as my mother called
him, for she still doubted at times whether he had really seen
the faces of saints and sanctuaries, this tranquil old soul,
perhaps he was waiting for nothing more than to tame my
mother, and then away he'd go, leaving the fireside, the set
table and the lamp that shone in the window on rainy nights.

One morning we caught him at the door, staring at the
scrubby copses that cut the horizon beyond the swollen
coulee. The rain was still falling. Soon it was mixed with
snow, and before the day's end the prairie, under its puffy
vestment, seemed quite round. Only once did we see him at
the door. But we knew he wanted to be on his way, as we had
known three weeks before, just from seeing him sit down and
sniff the smells of the house, that he wanted to stay. He was
just like a big, skinny dog we'd had when we were small, who

would beg to come in when the weather was bad and beg to go out when it was worse.

It was no use, my father's going back to the stories of Marcelline and France and Cousin Brault the fiddler, who left by himself for Montreal with his violin and played in orchestras there to the great shame of the family: Gustave's face had darkened. He looked at the door, nothing but the door, the one through which he had made such a joyous entrance. He looked nowhere else and seemed to be pining away each day. For we were witnesses to a strange phenomenon: the clothes my mother had given him seemed to be his own as long as he was happy to stay among us, but then we saw them collapse, hang loose about his shoulders, getting in his way. And what about the stories, the wonderful stories forever extinguished in his eyes! As the sky of our prairies is empty when all the wings have flown south, so Gustave's eyes grew bleak and, as it were, uninhabited. That was perhaps what we held against him most: not having any stories in reserve behind the farther mists of his pale smile.

One evening my father went so far as to offer him a little pay if he wanted to work. My mother showed no offence. Gustave's eyes were grateful, but he gave no other reply.

Next day he was gone. He must have slipped off at night, raising the latches cautiously. Farouche hadn't barked.

My mother flew into a rage. She ran to the silver drawer, to the relic box, to the crockery pot where the change was kept; nothing was missing anywhere. She counted the knives, the spoons, the candlesticks, but had to admit they were all there. Then she was even more humiliated.

"What did we do to make him leave like that?"

My father, for his part, inspected the barn, the granaries, the sheds. He came back discomfitted. The shadows on his mute face revealed a regret that did not fade away. From time

36

to time he sighed. At last one evening we heard him complaining, or accusing us: "We didn't receive him the way he deserved. He showed us: he went away."

But we had news of him the following year. In the mail one evening, along with the catalogue from the store in town and the weekly newspaper, was an envelope covered with an unknown handwriting, awkward and blotted with ink spots. My mother opened it at once. Leaning over her shoulder we read along with her. From the wet smell of the paper I cried out before reading a word: "It's from Gustave!"

A skip to the laborious and childish signature confirmed it. It was Gustave's.

He'd made it to Uncle Alfred's place in Saskatchewan and said he'd been asked to send regards. He said very kind things about the three girls, Emilie, Alma and Céline, whom my father, by the way, had described as hard to marry off: "Too fancy." From the lines a certain gaiety emanated. You could feel that Gustave was happy. No doubt he was telling his funniest stories in the evenings. A thin smell of tobacco clung to the paper. Crosses at the bottom were meant for kisses.

A little daring, this last familiarity! My mother didn't fail to be offended. My father grew cheerier and we often heard him prophesy in a satisfied tone: "You'll see, he'll be back one of these days."

The following year Gustave was in Alberta. He told us about it in a letter written at Uncle Edouard's place. Uncle Ed and Aunt Honora were working three-quarters of a section with their son. Gustave had helped with the harvest, which had been a good one. They had had him driving the truck, and he'd delivered the grain to the village. One girl was getting married this fall (he didn't say which one, and this unsettled point was the subject of many discussions among us). Another was taking orders. (My mother, to shut us up, said that could only be Paule, because of an old photo that showed her as rather scrawny, her eyes turned heavenward.) Anyway, all were well, including Gustave, except Honora who had stomach trouble. But he was sending for some of Ephrem Brabant's remedy to cure her. He didn't know yet if he'd spend the winter with the "relatives" or go and see a brother of Honora's who'd settled "across the big mountains."

My mother made a few objections, not so much to shake our convictions as to put her own to the test. Aunt Honora, who was such a cold, suspicious fish. . .how could she have given Gustave a welcome like this? That remained to be seen. You'd have thought my mother felt a little resentful.

We were certainly glad to get the news, in any case. Lazy about writing, we had never, for all our good resolutions, renewed a correspondence (which in fact had never begun) with our western uncles. And it seemed that Gustave, by taking this duty over, took our bad conscience with it.

This was all very well, but my mother took the opportunity of giving a little lesson to my father, indirectly, as she well knew how to do.

Her head thrown back, shaking a mat, she remarked one day: "I must say, there's strangers that have more family feeling than. . .than. . ."

My father refused to take offence. He smiled the serene smile of one whose confidence is sheltered from all doubt.

And so time passed. We had another letter six months later, not from British Columbia but from the Yukon, where Gustave vaguely gave us to understand he had turned trapper. Years passed. We might even have forgotten him had he not, by coming to see us long ago, awakened that mysterious thing: interest in one's family, that bewildering affinity that makes a Marcelline, unknown though she may be, less of a stranger than any other old woman in the village. Or, above all, if he hadn't left in our house the memory of so many places and things and people that still carried us through the long evenings, when boredom was not far and we grasped at dreams to drive it off. At those times, rising behind our hazy imaginings, the slightly drawling voice of Gustave would come back from the depths of our recollections.

We no longer talked of him, but thought of him often, each of us, in the evening when a shadow grew long on the road outside.

VI

He came back on a foggy, rainy night like the first one. And Farouche was the only one that knew him, from the smell of wet leaves and mud that his clothing gave off. They recognized each other, the man and the dog, the one perhaps luckier than the other because he had obeyed the mysterious call of the roads and the moonlit nights. But the man seemed weary. Leaning over the anxious dog, patting his head, you would have said he was advising him to appreciate the comfort of his kennel and perhaps even the benevolent servitude of the chain.

He straightened up, examined with the same slow, sad smile the roof of our house and the smoking chimney.

My mother uttered a few excited words: "Good Lord! It looks like. . ."

The man hesitated, then, as he had the first time, detoured around to tap on the back door.

I went to open it. His eyes, deep in their sockets, shone for a second. There was no more gaiety in those eyes, not even in their depths. The lustreless blue of water sleeping on the road after heavy storms!

But he exclaimed: "Ghislaine! I'd have known you anywhere, but my land, you've grown!"

I showed him into the big room. He followed me. He was just raising his arms in a great gesture to the reunited family when suddenly we saw him totter, then stagger against the stove and fall, his thin face turned toward us, a little spittle at his lips, his eyes fixed on the shadows like trickles of stagnant water.

My mother touched his reddened forehead. She said: "He has a high fever."

My father took Gustave's feet, my mother his shoulders, and they carried him to their bed.

Then his delirium began.

"I'm Barthélémy," he said. "Son of your brother Alcide. I come from Saint-Jerome. Yep, from Saint-Jerome."

Then he sighed.

"You've got to be friends with your folks, even if they're not always up to the mark."

Then again, in a wheezing voice, between coughing fits: "Come on! You don't know me? I'm Honoré, old man Phidime's boy, the one they thought was dead. I'm his Honoré!"

And suddenly he was muttering about tapers, the monstrance on the altar, the great piety of the world. In the middle of a brisk little laugh he exclaimed: "Good day to you, cousin Anastasie! Well, hello there!"

My father and mother exchanged a long look, then one after the other pulled a blanket over the sick man's body.

It snowed that night, and the next day too, and then another whole day. Then it blew. You could hear the coyotes that had ventured right to the doors of the barns, hear them howling and fighting over the carcass of a white hare that had fallen into their ambush. At times, from the growls that shook

41

Farouche's kennel, we concluded that a great wolf was stalking around the house. Powerful gusts swept the prairie, piled the snow high near the stables, sheds and all the buildings of the farm, which next morning would be half-buried. Snow was already up to our windows. Suddenly a great gust hurled itself against them as if to have a try through glass at blowing out our lamp, last visible sign of life struggling against the unleashed passion of the blizzard.

"No use talking," said my father. "We'll have to try and get out before all the roads are blocked. He could die, that fellow. At least we need some medicine."

He spoke with no warmth. You could feel that his grave affection for the poor wretch had not outlasted the confessions murmured in his delirium; he was being torn by an inner tempest as powerful as the one outside.

Just then, as if mysteriously aware of our concern and his own great danger, Gustave murmured among other unintelligible phrases: "Ephrem Brabant!"

Inspired, my mother fumbled in the pockets of his old overcoat hanging on a nail in the wall. She discovered a small brown bottle. On its label, the face with the white beard, that of the charlatan of Saint-Alphonse, seemed to us familiar and reassuring.

"It can't do him any harm, anyhow," said my mother.

She gave the poor man a gulp of the elixir.

"After all, he believed in it," she added.

My father was getting ready to go out just the same. He wrapped himself in a heavy coat with a fur collar and, to calm my mother, assured her he was just going to the nearest neighbour who had a phone.

My mother calculated: "Six miles there and back. I'll be worried."

A few minutes later we heard a faint sound of sleigh bells

whipped by the wind, then the horse whinnying as it plunged past the fence into an immense, tumultuous tempest.

Gustave was quieter after he had swallowed Ephrem Brabant's remedy. Soon he was sleeping deeply, his hands open on the white sheet.

"Now who'd have thought it!" my mother sighed.

Several times she went to sniff at the few drops of brown syrup left in the bottle.

"Just because he believed in it."

Her remark, however, seemed to refer less to the remedy than to a possible thought that arose in her, illuminating her solitary wonderment. She resisted it still at times, as you could see from her restive look; then, with a little shrug of her shoulders, she seemed to give in to the undeniable evidence.

The hours passed. The sick man was still asleep. My mother had finally dozed off. But, waking suddenly, she looked at the clock with growing anguish. Then she struggled to keep awake, and watched over Gustave as she had watched over us, her children, through our illnesses.

Then came the crunching of the cutter's runners in the snow, as if it were still far off, though it was in fact close by the house. A little later my father came in. He was pale, despite the cold, and in a shaking rage.

"How is he?" he asked.

My mother pointed to Gustave, sleeping, and indicated that it was all right to talk.

Then my father turned on her violently as if he were going to accuse her: "The very idea! . . . Albertine. . . . Who'd have thought it? Do you know the police may be here tomorrow because of him?"

"What! He's not a criminal? Oh, no!" stammered my mother, her hands fluttering to her heart.

"No. Maybe worse."

"Is he crazy? Sick?" she asked, pressing her hands to her heaving breasts.

"No. But I'd just as soon it was that."

"What then? Tell me, Arthur."

My father strode across the room, darting wounded glances to one side and the other. His thick overcoat, which he had forgotten to take off, gave an impressive form to his shadow on the wall.

"Oh," he shouted, with lively rancour, "he'd be just as well off dead, that fellow. Imagine, Albertine, and you looked after him so well! Imagine, he passed himself off for a Lafrenière at the Lafrenières below the big hill. And for a Poirier at the Poiriers. And so on. He hasn't one name, that man, he has ten, twenty, as many families as he likes."

"What then?" asked my mother. She had grown strangely calm.

"An impostor!" my father exploded. "Don't you realize, Albertine? An impostor!"

He tried to control his voice: "Somebody reported him. The police have started an inquiry. When people find out he's here. . ."

"What then, Arthur?"

My mother had taken up her stand at the door of the bedroom as if to forbid all entry. Tiny as she was, when she stood this way, her head high, her eyes flashing with determination, not many would have dared defy her.

"Well?" she said. "Don't we know what to say? Don't we know it?" she repeated, questioning each of us in turn with her clear, open gaze.

Suddenly the violence that had seized my father was broken. He seemed infinitely tired. Almost feeling his way, he sought out his chair in the corner by the fire and sank down in it. And at last we understood the disenchantment, worse than anger, that he had to bear. A Marcelline who could laugh and dance at her second wedding; Eustache, attached to the memory of his parents; a tender, affectionate Philomène; these characters, like a mirage that had for some time fed my father's dreams, had already disappeared from before his eyes. They were replaced by a dried-up, hardened little woman, by the bad son who had deceived his parents, by Philomène, frightful and graceless. In my father's eyes we saw the return of that absence of love with which he had had to live for so long.

"Good gracious now!" my mother said in a curiously persuasive tone. "Who's to prove it isn't true? He has to be somebody's relative. What's to prove to us it isn't true?"

Next morning Gustave awoke practically cured. He accepted the warm clothing my mother had taken from the trunks for him. He thanked her without effusiveness. You'd have thought he'd left a few of his things with us, and was grateful to get them back clean and mended. Gradually our wrath, our shame at having liked him, quieted down.

That day the sky swept the snow away with great waves of sunlight. The buildings, the cutters with their shafts pointed skyward, the buckets and barrels, all our everyday things, projected only the flimsiest of shadows in the immense plain all trembling with light. In the distance, on the hardened crust of the prairie, tiny tracks made their way toward the woods. At dawn, when the storm grew still, the wolves and coyotes had again sought the refuge of the trees.

Gustave was getting ready to go. He went to the door, downcast, but paused, his hand on the latch. My mother was preparing a splendid stew of jack rabbit and beef.

"There's no rush," she said, paying no attention to my father's silence. "You were a sick man. There's no rush at all."

Gustave made a despairing gesture with his arms. Then a shiver passed through his whole body. He seemed to be struggling against the temptation of warmth and the odour of the stew. Had some echo of our words of yesterday floated up in his memory? Or was it his old mania taking over again? He began to lift the latch.

"I suppose you have to get along to see some relatives?"

My mother had spoken in a friendly and reassuring voice. The man pricked up his ears. His stooped shoulders straightened. He looked back at the room. Greedily, as if to make a memory of it, he contemplated a ray of sunlight slanting through it, delicately lighting up the steam from the pots simmering on the stove. Finally he glanced up at my mother. His old eyes with their worn gaze were shining again.

"Yes," he said.

"Well! And which way are you heading this time?"

"I have some folks on my mother's side. . .in Ontario. . ." he began uncertainly.

"Would that be down Hawkesbury way?" asked my mother, with every sign of lively interest. "They say there's a lot of our people there still speak French."

She had thrown a shawl over her shoulders. She went with the man past the threshold. She encouraged him with her eyes. He went off, walking backward a few steps, as if he couldn't decide whether to give up my mother's accepting gaze. Then he turned to face the naked, empty plain.

Farouche, straining at his leash, was whining, almost choking himself in the attempt to leave with that miserable silhouette.

"Quiet, Farouche, quiet!" said my mother.

Then she did something so simple, so splendid. Cupping her hands to her mouth, she shouted loudly into the wind, her apron flying around her: "Take care! Take good care. . .Cousin Gustave!"

Did he hear? Perhaps. In any case, he had cut a branch in our garden for a walking stick.

Where Will You Go, Sam Lee Wong?

Where Will You Go, Sam Lee Wong?

Had his life begun in a land of hills? At times he fancied he found their contours in himself, intimate as breathing. Then he would gaze downward to see them better, in self-communion with his memory. Vague, rounded shapes, half-blurred, gathered along an uncertain horizon, then dissolved. Did the vision come from a recollection of real hills, or from some picture that had struck his imagination? In a sense they were more real than his own existence had ever seemed, whether in Canton or Fuchow or elsewhere: a yellow face among an infinity of yellow faces; at times, a face borne only on a sea of crowds, noise and hunger; also, it was true, amid the stream of humans, a small, barely audible voice that dared to call itself Me.

A stevedore among clouds of stevedores, and at the docks one grain of humanity, a particle of the dust of life. What could he remember as being his except perhaps his name, and even that was common as air around the waterfront. Only in the dark recess where he slept—a hole in the wall—could he escape from the multitude that worried him along.

At last, one day he came to a kind of personal conclusion: there are too many of us in China. Couldn't one live more at ease in other parts of the world? He heard tell of a country as vast as all the provinces of China put together, but almost empty of all human presence. So much room, so few people, was it possible? Sam Lee Wong listened. . . . He could hardly believe such tales. . . .

Nonetheless, a few months later, with almost a thousand of his countrymen, he embarked on a ship leaving for that land of youth and hope. Gathered on deck, the Asians kept watch for its appearance with all their souls, but with their usual expression of humility, and eyes so weary you might have thought them devoid of interest even in their own destiny.

But it was then that Sam Lee Wong, leaning on the railing, found a firmer grasp on the tenuous thread that linked him to the ancient hills in the back of his memory. He remembered rice bowls filled to the brim. He recalled a little coat made of several layers of quilted cotton. He even thought he glimpsed a little boy with chubby cheeks, comfortable in the warm coat. Was there some connection between Sam Lee Wong and this apparently well-fed child? Sam Lee Wong wondered about it, staring perplexed at the heaving water. But the ocean, which by some mystery had brought back a forgotten scene, now bore it off again on its heavy swell.

At last they could see a shoreline trimmed with high mountains. The sight of them recalled again to Sam Lee Wong the relief of his ancient hills. This time he saw them leaning, all in the same direction, like a row of old trees in the wind. He could see, without understanding how it all belonged together, an offered bowl of rice, protective hilltops, a coat of quilted cotton; and he set foot in Vancouver, still

52

in a press of his own countrymen, and far from persuaded that there was space here that could leave you breathless, and yet so few mouths to feed.

In Vancouver, the Sons of the Orient Aid Society took them in charge. For each one it tried to discover, in the breadth and length of this almost unpeopled country, the spot that might be most suitable. They were made to take a course of several weeks in English to at least learn its rudiments. Each immigrant also received a loan to get him started. Paid back, little by little, the money would be lent again to some new son of the Orient arriving, so to speak, on the heels of his predecessor. Thus there would be no drying-up of the thin flow of money or the thin trickle, tightly controlled, of Chinese immigration.

In fact the Aid Society had very few jobs to offer the little yellow men arriving from Canton, Peking or Manchuria. They almost all, therefore, ended up in the same odd occupation. In the distances of the endless plains, flat and without contours, minuscule villages had sprung up ten or fifteen years before. If they were big enough to contain one Chinaman they put him in a restaurant. If a village were even more flourishing and could afford a second Chinaman, the latter of necessity opened a laundry. That's how it went in these poor villages, almost deprived of all tradition except that of always putting their newcomers from Asia into the same occupations. The astonishing thing was that the Chinese laundrymen soon acquired the reputation of being the best in the world. As for the restaurants, it is less certain that they were the first in their field. Yet who but a Chinese with nothing to lose would have opened a café in one of these scrawny little towns where catching a single customer was a major feat!

In the headquarters of the Sons of the Orient Aid Society, Sam Lee Wong patiently studied the map of this immense country with its unfamiliar names, among which he had a choice almost as disconcerting as the map itself. What would be the new countenance of solitude? Would it be still more intense than in the teeming crowd? Or just the same as ever? Sam Lee Wong's gaze wandered over the map's puzzling spaces and was truly at a loss where to stop.

"Take your pick!" they told him. "Here! There! Anywhere! It's your choice, Sam Lee Wong. There's nothing to stop you."

Perhaps, tired of his own hesitation, he was about to put his finger on one or the other of the signs scattered across the map, when one of his compatriots charitably pointed out that such and such an area was not really to be recommended. A little chain of hills, wild and barren, rose from the plain. Most likely the soil was poor there, and business would suffer.

Hills!

Sam Lee Wong's eyelids fluttered as if he had heard someone softly call his name.

He pretended to study intently this portion of the map which was not to be recommended. In fact he was trying to see the elusive hills of his most distant memories. They alone managed to endow him with a kind of identity and the feeling that even here in Canada he was still somehow Sam Lee Wong. A moment earlier he had begun to doubt it, as he searched hopelessly among the undecipherable names on the map. He had had the impression that he was no one, just a fragment of being, nothing but a wandering thought stranded here, without the support of soul or body.

Now he was able to place himself within his personality and life, because of a horizon and the recurring image of a steaming bowl of rice.

And so he put his finger on the map at the place said to be so unexpectedly traversed by a little chain of hills.

That was how he learned that he had chosen Saskatchewan, and that he had attached his life to a village therein which, curiously enough, was called Horizon.

II

And in fact that's about all there was to it: a horizon so distant, so lonely, so poignant, that your heart was gripped by it again and again.

Luckily, a chain of little hills far to the right put a stop on that one side to the flight of the landscape. As the village lay perfectly open, wherever you were you couldn't miss seeing those surprising hills, and, on finding them again each morning, feeling in them a kind of refuge against the dizziness produced after a time by the flat, unmoving plain.

It was when the sun went down among their folds that the hills, filled with a strange light, exercised the strongest fascination on the people down below in the stagnant village. That was how things were between hills and village when, one September day, Sam Lee Wong, his wicker suitcase in his hand, got off the train and set foot in Horizon.

The day was hot and windy. When the train had gone, Sam Lee Wong, alone on the wooden platform, looked like a human being set down there by sleight of hand.

The Society had dressed him in occidental clothes. Beneath

a broad, black felt hat, in a light gabardine, his frail neck choking in a flowered tie, Sam Lee Wong seemed less than ever to belong. He almost gave the impression of waiting until fate would see her way clear to taking him by the collar once again.

The wind raised powdered earth in eddies of dust. Not a soul was about in the village. Even the stationmaster behind his dusty window didn't trouble to raise his nose from the report he was skimming.

Sam Lee Wong, supremely conspicuous in the very centre of the small, wooden platform between the station and the dark-red water tank, might as well have been invisible, for no one appeared to see him. He stayed motionless for a moment, not even thinking to set down his suitcase. He looked at the space surrounding him. Finally, after leaving his case by the empty bench in front of the station, he crossed the rails, with their rustling border of tall weeds, and then the road, and came to the board sidewalk.

He hesitated a moment as to which way to go, then started toward the plain on the right. He walked slowly, noiselessly, looking around but with furtive glances as if he didn't yet dare take a good long look.

Apart from the beginnings of a side street at right angles – only two houses were on it – the whole village was strung out along the highway, and the wind rushed through incessantly, finding no obstacle in its path.

At the sidewalk's end, Sam Lee Wong gazed out at the prairie which went on and on, without a wrinkle or an undulation. Two more houses, farther along, might belong to the village, but after that it was emptiness.

Sam Lee Wong retraced his steps. Now he was facing the little hills that rose up two or three miles away. The moment they entered the landscape it grew less desolate, less overpowering. A touch of fancy, a certain grace, you might have said, came at last to the frightful stretch of flatness.

This time Sam Lee Wong went a little more quickly and looked more boldly on either side. In any case, he now had a good notion of this village where his fate had brought him. The most important thing in Horizon was beyond a doubt those two strange towers that gave off a smell of grain, near the railway station, with enormous letters standing out in white. Sam Lee Wong had already understood that this was where the village stored its riches, enough to see it through any famine; and the descendant of hungry generations stared with infinite respect at the tall letters making up the words: Saskatchewan Wheat Pool.

A strange thing: apart from the station, the water tank and the other railway outbuildings, all in the same dark red, the whole village lay not only along the highway but on one side of it, facing the endless fields, as if prepared to wait till eternity for the curtain to go up.

Sam Lee Wong was now taking in details that he'd noted only from the corner of his eye the first time around. He recognized a tall house surmounted by a cross. Before the door a man in black walked to and fro reading a book, never interrupting his reading to glance at the passer-by. Unless he was peeking, like Sam Wong, who today seemed to look about freely only when people's attention was elsewhere.

Then the school set free a troop of excited children who started playing football. This time Sam Lee Wong stopped and stared. He stayed for a long moment on the edge of the walk following the children's play, while his silent laughter accompanied their rowdiness. It was the first time since he arrived on this continent that he had stopped to contemplate a spectacle from which he himself was not totally excluded. And yet the playing children seemed to pay no attention to his presence, obvious though it was. Perhaps its very oddity made it inaccessible. After awhile a young girl appeared in the school doorway and rang a hand bell. The children went back inside. Sam Lee Wong continued on his way. He began seriously looking for what he needed.

Not much, in fact: an abandoned house, even a little decrepit if that made it cheaper, no more than a shelter, in short; but well located. And that wasn't as easy as you might think, for with the children gone and the sound of their voices silent, all seemed empty again.

With time Sam Lee Wong was to grow used to the idea of a village so swallowed in silence that it seemed deserted; with little grey houses, morose, from which a sound, if one escaped, was at once swept off by the wind and smothered in its perpetual wailing. He would get used to this kind of solitude, but for the moment he simply thought that everyone had left.

Just to be sure, he put his thin face to the window of a house that was particularly lifeless. His hands beside his eyes to intercept the light and see inside, he gave it a searching going-over until, to his profound stupefaction, he met the gaze of someone staring at him with a surprise as great as his own, perhaps even indignation. He drew back instinctively, then pressed his face to the glass again to offer in apology – whether to the dark pane or the astonished face – an immense and humble smile.

This smile, by the way, was now to become a part of Sam Lee Wong and appear for every purpose on his melancholy face. Making-do as a language? Because there was no other way he could be understood? Whatever the answer, this broad smile on a sad Chinese face was to astonish no one here. A Chinaman who didn't smile – that might have shocked them.

After going over the whole village twice, Sam Lee Wong

was able to count the shanties that were really empty: three in all. One of them tempted him more than the others, though it was in wretched condition. The façade had a curious bulge, as though it had long ago half given way to some internal pressure. It must have been used as a granary, for there was still a smell of wheat about. In fact, Sam Lee Wong could see through the window that grain still lay in a pile on the floor. But this house with its smell of wheat was right across from the station, at the point of heaviest traffic in the village, if traffic there ever should be. Moreover, it had an unusually large window that took up a good half of the front. Sam Lee Wong didn't mind the façade either. It gave the shack a Far West look such as he had seen on postcards.

Pensive, Sam Lee Wong saw himself partly reflected in the dirty window pane, and he also saw a kind of future taking shape there. Business couldn't turn out so badly, even in this sleepy village, with such a big window to attract the public. When Sam Lee Wong would finally hear the history of the shack he'd be even more drawn to it, for before being a granary, at a time when the village had achieved an almost sensational boom, it had housed the branch of a bank, and this was the reason for the big window. Then it had been turned into an office for the municipality, and that was when they'd installed a counter dividing its space laterally. When Sam Lee Wong, growing used to the dim light inside, saw the counter, he was almost as happy as he had been about the window. No need to search farther. Everything he could wish for was here.

The hard thing to find out would be: who was the owner of this former municipal office? And when he had found the present owner (a farmer who lived at the edge of the village), how to make him understand that he wanted to rent the ruin? At last the deal was made. For six dollars a month and repairs the office-granary was Sam Lee Wong's.

Before nightfall he had moved in. On his way back from the owner's house he had bought a pail, some soap and a broom. Late that night, a feeble lamp on the counter lit the comings and goings of Sam Lee Wong, his fine duds removed and replaced by a kind of apron-robe, sweeping and tidying as if he were already mysteriously at home. Whether it was the room that seemed to grow larger and emptier as he tidied it, or the enormous shadow moving on the walls, the fact is that the few passing villagers who cast a glance inside drew back in their turn, perhaps embarrassed at coming unexpectedly upon this too-naked image of solitude. Why, of a sudden, in their already solitary midst, should there be this Chinaman, unconnected, destitute? They went home trying to forget the picture they had seized in passing, of a man setting up house much as a bird makes its nest, at the world's whim.

On his clothes rolled into a pillow at the back of the great, empty room, Sam Lee Wong laid down his head and slept. Elsewhere in the village people were also retiring for the night, and all had a moment of afterthought, sharpened as it often is before the regrets and bad memories of the day drift off. For at the moment when she rang the bell the schoolteacher had indeed seen the Chinaman standing halfway along the sidewalk; and the priest between two phrases of his breviary had glimpsed him out of the corner of an eye; and of course the Saskatchewan Wheat Pool dealer, who from the top of the grain elevator had the best view of the stranger's comings and goings; and Pete Finlinson, section boss for the railway, from his residence, an old freight car set flat among the thistles close by the tracks; and many others whom the timidity of the Chinese had somehow frozen – or what was it then that kept them from making some gesture of kindness? Little by little, night stretched across the isolated village, in

61

the distance of the naked plains. The wind rose and rattled at the flimsy frame houses and blew dust along the main street, where three lampposts, far apart, kept their reflective watch. What was the meaning of Sam Lee Wong's appearance in Horizon? Another unanswered enigma. No doubt, at last and luckily, they all slipped into slumber, Sam Lee Wong among them, his head on his roll of clothes.

A few days later, in the middle of the big window, now washed and shining, you could read, drawn in soap, the following advertisement:

RESTAURANT SAM LEE WONG
GOOD FOOD
MEALS AT ALL HOURS

III

Some time later, on a fine, dry morning, old man Smouillya happened along in the front of the café. For twenty years or more he'd been searching for a sympathetic ear in which to pour the too-incredible story of his life, of which you couldn't make head or tail. As a very young man he had left his village in the French Pyrenees and wakened one fine day in Horizon without ever really knowing how it had come about. A mountaineer transplanted into this naked plain! From then on, all his efforts had been directed toward getting out. But misfortunes had piled up and swamped him. Finally he had lost everything – his land and buildings, for debts; then his wife, from illness; and at last his children. All he had left was a shack at the end of the village. There he passed the winter, in such filth that you couldn't see your way around. When spring came he would move out pots and pans and camp beside his house, never setting foot in it for the three or four months of decent weather. Always half-drunk – on his home-made chokecherry wine, some said, or under the influence of a strange and tenacious aberration – you couldn't understand a word of old Smouillya's wanderings. Some people affirmed, however, that they'd come upon him by surprise, sitting on the ground, his back turned to the houses, weeping silently as he stared at the distant hills fired by the setting sun. But was he really weeping? Or was it his catarrh that left his face running with water?

Well, this old Smouillya happened by the restaurant. In the doorway was Sam Lee Wong, all smiles.

"Good molnin! Nice molnin!" he said to old Smouillya.

The latter, in astonishment, stopped cold. For years no one had given him more than a nod, for fear that if you even said good-day he'd take you by the sleeve and start into his endless monologue of which you wouldn't understand a word. Even in his youth he'd been barely comprehensible, what with his strong Basque accent and a speech defect. But now that he'd lost his teeth, and little jets of spit whistled from his mouth, and chronic asthma wheezed in his lungs…! It's very trying, one must admit, listening to someone tell you with great enthusiasm something important, perhaps his life story, perhaps his troubles, and not catch a single word or even know which expression to put on, pitying or happy! It was to spare themselves this embarrassment that people gradually, without really meaning to be unkind, started avoiding old Smouillya.

"Nice days todays," Sam Lee Wong said chattily.

Now old Smouillya could understand Sam Lee Wong. Understood by so few himself, there was practically no jargon or patois that he didn't succeed in deciphering.

In his impossible accent he replied: "Why, yes, a fine day, Son of the Celestial Empire."

That seemed to please Sam Lee Wong, whose smile grew even broader.

The aroma of sausages and fried onions drifted out from the back of the restaurant. Old Smouillya sniffed, strongly tempted. On this, his very first day in business, Sam Lee Wong discovered in himself an extreme facility for reading the faces and gestures of men. He quickly said, "Come. . .come. . .come" – moving back to let Smouillya in, and pointing with a courteous gesture to one of the two lonely little tables covered with oilcloth.

"Sit, sit, sit," he said, then ran to turn the sausages in the pan. They were already cooked and re-cooked.

Was it the glow of the fire that brought up from the depths of his slanted eyes an expression of tranquility? In any case, the Chinese seemed that morning to have found his place as a restaurant-keeper. Old Smouillya, for his part, was barely seated before he took on the airs of a customer, with just a touch of superiority over the one who serves, attenuated by polite camaraderie. At the same time the old fellow examined the place and nodded approvingly at the transformation effected in the old granary. It didn't feel in the least like a granary now, and still less like a bank. In fact, it had everything that constitutes a restaurant in a western village, from the two little tables with their four chairs each and a highly typical greasy smell, to the flies that buzzed around so gaily.

No sooner was Smouillya served than he attacked the sausages, spearing them three at a time on his knife. It made the trip to his mouth only twice and the lot had disappeared.

His meal ended, he took a toothpick from the table, poked it about inside his mouth, and ended up chewing it. Then, leaning back in his chair, he began to tell Sam Lee Wong, who stood deferentially before him in his white apron, the story that no one in the village had fully understood: first the drought years; then the wheat rust, which ruined two of his best harvests; finally the seizure of his machinery. All this he told with spittle flying in every direction and a rattling deep in the lungs, but also with a kind of leisureliness, of unexpected relaxation, because for the first time he was heard out with patient silence, and in his listener's eye he could read neither the desire to flee nor the impulse to plug his ears. This was so pleasantly surprising that Smouillya made his story longer and more picturesque than ever. For he didn't lack education, imagination, the power of invention or telling imagery; and perhaps the most painful thing in his life was that he had never been able to make these gifts apparent to anyone. With a new serenity and smiling almost as broadly as Sam Lee Wong, Smouillya finally managed to tell someone all his troubles.

But, he said, they were just about at an end. He was expecting some money, it was bound to arrive any day now. Then he'd pay his debts and go back to live in his country, in the mountains. There, beside the French Pyrenees, said Smouillya, he'd find his place; if not to live, at least to die in peace.

Suddenly the old man realized that he was in a public place, that the Chinese had obligations to other possible customers, and he hastily began fumbling in his pockets, which he knew were empty. With an energetic gesture, shaking his head, Sam Lee Wong put an end to the fumbling. Smouillya willingly got the message that Sam Lee Wong was refusing to be paid this one time and considered his first customer as his guest, for good luck.

"Oh, well, in that case I'll accept," said Smouillya magnanimously. "But from now on, oh! Son of the Celestial Empire, take note of the meals I undertake to eat in your café. Write them all down, for before I go back to my native

66

Pyrenees I'll pay all my debts, starting with you, you man of gentle heart!"

Sam Lee Wong accompanied the old man to the door. He too seemed to have something on his mind, something he wanted to relate. His gaze was an inward one. He tried and tried, and finally with infinite pains and trouble put a few words together: "China too many people, much people. Here big, not much people. Everywhere Chinaman all alone. World very funny. Little hills, over there, good!"

From being understood by no one, Smouillya had come to understand even stray cats, and that was enough for him to grasp the longing of the café-keeper. He put one arm around Sam Lee Wong's thin shoulder. He encouraged him. What was more, until other customers started to come he undertook to drop in almost every day – on his days off, of course – to occupy his place in the restaurant. That would bring the others along. Nothing like a good example! He would even spread the word about Sam Lee Wong's good cooking, and soon they'd be there in droves; and when the two of them had made their fortune they could go back to their own countries, he to his majestic Pyrenees and Sam Lee Wong to the little round hills of his childhood.

He kept his word. It was very seldom, as long as the weather was good, that he didn't turn up for his midday meal, for which he paid provisionally by telling of the world as he saw it: a tremendous merry-go-round where no one ever understood anyone else. There was nothing like mountains for saving mankind, mountains which by their nobility and unchanging nature obliged the species to arrest its endless chase.

He didn't stop coming until the severe cold forced him to move back into his shack, where he stayed for the winter. Lacking his chokecherry wine, he lost appetite and hope.

Then the profile of the Pyrenees grew distant, distant in his mind. Sometimes, taking his head in his hands, he would shake it as if trying to bring back some consoling image; for in his dark cabin, its windows boarded up to keep him from freezing alive, he could truly no longer see where to get the money to pay his debts and buy his ticket home.

IV

With the months and then the years, Sam Lee Wong's business prospered in a small way. Jim Farrell, the stationmaster, had a big argument with his young wife, Margot. She took the train for Moose Jaw one Thursday morning and was never seen again.

After a week of mortification Farrell had had enough of fried eggs three times a day, alone, at the corner of his table. He came over to try the food at the "Chink's place," as he called it, and must have liked it, for he came back. Perhaps best of all, he could say what he liked about women and not risk being quoted around town. Or perhaps he was too drunk those days to care much.

To hear him talk, they were crazy. All of them, crazy! Spenders, too, and extravagant, and man-crazy! Anybody said you couldn't get on without them was a fool. No sir, them silly articles, good riddance to them, a fellow could breathe easy at last!

At the times when Farrell was pouring out his most whole-hearted resentment, Sam Lee Wong made himself as invisible as possible and finally almost disappeared in his own restaurant. But one evening when Farrell was more dishevelled than usual, he addressed himself directly to the Chink.

"You, Chinaman, darn lucky not have woman!"

Though he still didn't have a big vocabulary, Sam Lee Wong would have learned to express himself quite well if people had only helped a little. He learned quickly. But they went on talking to him as if he were retarded. And he, out of politeness, so as not to shame those who spoke in this way, would answer in much the same style.

"Yes, Wong lucky no woman!" he acquiesced.

At that time there was a very cruel immigration law regulating the entry of Chinese immigrants into Canada. Men – a few thousand of them a year – were admitted, but no women, no children. Later the law was made more humane. In those western villages lost in boredom and tawdry dreams, in those same little restaurants with their smell of grease, you could henceforth see beside each Sam Lee Wong a little woman, probably on the plump side, doing her best to help him; and sometimes a swarm of yellow children pushing around in the back of the café; and if all of these were still outsiders in the village, at least they were outsiders together. But in Sam Lee Wong's time a Chinese woman beside him was as unthinkable as the King of England coming to Horizon.

"Yes, good no woman," Sam Lee Wong approved sadly.

Sometimes, rediscovering the vague memory of the quilted cotton coat and the bowl of rice, he also fancied he glimpsed a woman's loving face. His mother? An older sister? He didn't know.

Soon his two little tables with their four places each were filled at seven in the morning, at midday sharp, and six o'clock at night. From one meal to the next the smell of bacon grease had no time to escape into the distance. The overflow reached the sidewalk and built up there. It became a part of Horizon, like the dominant sour smell escaping from the tavern Saturday evenings, like the acrid perfume of wheat when they were filling the Saskatchewan Wheat Pool elevators.

After Farrell, Sam Lee Wong acquired Pete Finlinson as a regular. A heavy-set man with thick, straw-coloured hair, the Icelander had grown tired of coming back from the tour of his railway section and going straight to his freight-car home, feeling literally as if he were on the rails. He too began to like Sam Lee Wong's fried food, or perhaps more Sam Lee Wong himself, for though Pete was not a man who made friends, there he'd be, long after he'd eaten, watching the Chinaman's perpetual comings and goings. In fact no one, not Farrell, not even Finlinson who after all spent hours in his corner in the café, could say that he had ever seen the Chinaman sitting down.

Motionless at times, yes, but sitting in one of his own chairs? Never! What the devil kept this little man on the go all the time? (Between his four walls, of course. He almost never went beyond them.) Inside only, then. But there he went, trot, trot, trot, as if he had a thousand chores to do at once, though his place remained as greasy as ever.

"Where do you come from, Wong?" asked Finlinson one evening when he happened to feel talkative.

Sam Lee Wong opened his mouth in a vast smile. He pointed beyond the plain. "Far!"

"I well believe you. Indeed it must be from far. There's nobody here doesn't come from some end of the earth. Me, it's Iceland, and I came all this way to turn into a section hand in Horizon. Isn't that a hell of a funny story? Here we are, you from Far, like you say, and me from Iceland, Farrell

71

from the Isle of Man, Smouillya from the Pyrenees and Jacob from old Quebec. . . ."

Then he forgot how strange it all was and began dreaming aloud about Iceland. It was the smells he missed most, smells of iodine and fish and the open sea, penetrating the whole life of the immense island.

Then the Saskatchewan Wheat Pool dealer got the habit of passing time in the café when he was tipsy, rather than face his wife, Lilly.

Yes, Sam Lee Wong had a lot of strange customers, more of them lonely and discontented than happy, and it seemed he took pains to fit their mood, though perhaps that was not so hard for him.

But when he at last acquired an ice-cream cooler, his café began to be invaded on Saturday nights by the young people from nearby farms and hamlets, sitting around for hours and making a splendid racket. The whole atmosphere changed. Instead of lamentations the air was filled with hearty laughter and endless jokes. It was then that Sam Lee Wong installed two tables with high-backed benches attached, on one side of the room. When the gangs of young couples came in Sam would invite them, with a gesture and a smile, to be seated in these booths. They would occupy them for hours on end, sucking away at the straws of their milkshakes or cream sodas, their feet and hands seeking each other out beneath the table.

Sam Lee Wong served these customers with perhaps a little more alacrity than he had demonstrated to those who complained about women or life in general. But this preference, if it really existed, was barely measurable. In fact, the only one to reproach him about it was Smouillya, who was unusually sensitive.

"What's the idea, spoiling these snot-nosed brats? You can't even come here and think in peace and quiet, the way we used to. What a racket they make!"

"Tut-tut," said Sam Lee Wong, allowing himself to make a mild reproach. "You young one time. You not remember?"

"Oh, that's so long ago," sighed the old man. "So long ago! And anyway, in our time we weren't bold like this lot."

"Always old men say that," Sam Lee Wong observed.

Just the same, there was soon no room for doubt that he put up with just about anything from the young folk, a real shivaree going on till all hours, glasses broken, Coke splattered on the tables. But with the same impassive face he had also put up with Farrell's grumbling, or the chronic belching of one Charrette, or the ponderous reminiscences of the Icelander. What hadn't he put up with? At times you might even surmise that he was the one in the village who cramped people's style the least, and that, consequently, he knew them better than anyone in the world.

V

Month by month Sam Lee Wong came closer to paying off his debt to the Sons of the Orient Aid Society. Smouillya, never very particular in money questions, openly tried to dissuade him from undue haste in acquitting his debt or even from worrying about it at all. The Aid Society had lots of money, he'd say. It could wait for Sam's. It could wait indefinitely. What was more, it would never sue a bad creditor, for that would reveal its racket to the public.

Sam Lee Wong was stubbornly deaf to these arguments. As he saw it, some poor Chinese in Vancouver, or maybe even in Canton, was waiting for that money to come and set up business in the Canadian prairies. Not for anything in the world would he be the one to block or slow down the trickle of immigration.

"You're crazy, you know," the Basque would go at him time and again, with a touch of resentment, as if the Chinaman had thrown away good money that somehow should have gone Smouillya's way. "Just be sure you keep a bit for yourself, if you want us to go back to our home countries

74

some day, you and me. You in your coffin, all doctored up, and me on my two legs if things go my way. You'll make the trip in a special boat," he explained, "fitted up special to bring the deceased back to the Celestial Empire. Some kind of a refrigerator boat, I expect."

Then he'd come back to his theme for the hundredth time.

"But if they don't treat you right, according to the deal, you're in no shape to complain. And it's a poor deal, at that. If you can't go back alive, why in the sam hill do you want to go back dead?"

Sam Lee Wong had given him the answer time and again: it was to be reunited with his ancestors.

"But you never even saw them!"

"They'll know me," Sam Lee Wong would say.

"It's just this crazy idea of yours and all you ex-coolies," Smouillya would go on, "this idea of going back to China to be buried, it's making your crooked countrymen rich in Vancouver. When you're dead you've no comeback against their tricks. I hear they pile you up in the hold like cordwood. And they hold the shipment till they get a payload!"

Never mind! Sam Lee Wong contributed a little money every month toward his eternal retirement fund.

"You write. You send money for me, same as always."

Smouillya had a fine, clear and delicate hand, which Sam Lee Wong admired as much as the frost patterns on his windows. And no matter how the man went off on endless digressions or lost the thread of his own remarks in conversation, when he wrote, his sentences were concise and to the point. This was the old Basque's one priceless gift, and only Sam Lee Wong was aware of it, for only he had called upon it. The old man wrote his letters for him, and orders for sausages and supplies, and the tireless expressions of gratitude that accompanied each instalment of money to Vancouver.

When Smouillya brought these extraordinary letters and read them to Sam Lee Wong, the latter went into ecstasies. He even stopped smiling, lost in a kind of blissful gravity.

"It's me said that?" he would ask at the finest passages.

"That was you. Anyhow, that's what you wanted to say, oh Son of the Celestial Empire. Isn't it? For you and yours were always given a great gift of self-expression. That's what I read, anyway, in accounts of travels to ancient Cathay. Have you read them?"

"No," said Sam Lee Wong, regretfully. "I will know my people when I am dead."

Then he would admire his name, which when written occidental-style looked very impressive indeed, as Smouillya decorated his capitals with a kind of flying stroke, as if they were about to take wing.

"That's me?" Sam Lee Wong would ask, overwhelmed at last by emotion.

"Well, I should say! Look here: Sam Lee Wong, Esquire."

"I'm esquire?" the café owner asked.

"Just like me! Just like everybody!"

Sometimes on these occasions the memory of the hills before Horizon's hills came back to Sam Lee Wong. A woman's face emerged from the mist of years. He felt a kind of continuity with certain lost things, he wasn't sure exactly what. In a burst of gratitude he cried out one day: "You, Smouillya, not owe meals eight years. You owe four years, no more."

Always magnanimous, Smouillya, sputtering in all directions, protested vehemently: "Never on your life! I owe you eight years. All right, take off one year for secretarial services. Maybe another year for cogitation on your best interests. And take off the days my asthma kept me from looking after your business. But don't you worry. It's all written down on the back of my calendar."

Then, forgetting it was only yesterday he'd been counting on Sam Lee Wong's savings to see them both back in their native lands, he added: "With what I owe you, you're sure of a ride back in a first-class coffin. It's as good as money in the bank."

And he would sigh: "At least you, you've got some money in the bank!"

Sam Lee Wong, not quite as innocent as all that, gave in to a significant little smile one day as the Basque was harping on the same old theme.

Smouillya, catching the smile in mid-flight, was offended. He struck the rickety table with a fist.

"Money in the bank, I tell you! Your money, whenever you want it!"

VI

And now a great drought, just like the ones that had driven Sam Lee Wong and so many like him from their homeland, swept down upon Horizon and the surrounding country. On the plains it traced an enormous circle haunted by the lament of scorching air in which you could almost hear the plant life crackle, where you could watch the burnt earth crumble and turn to powder. In the rich landscape it singled out this ring of misery that came to be called the Desert Bowl. Within it, indeed, nothing was left but arid desert!

Farmers left home, leaving all behind them except a few skin-and-bone animals half dead of thirst, led away behind wagons or cars driven at a snail's pace. Nothing could have been more strange than to glimpse through the flying dust these weird processions, dimly seen and lost at once in the opaque daylight.

Doors everywhere, of houses, barns and stables, flapped half unhinged in the wind. Their banging, and the occasional squeaking of a pulley or the cry of some bird flying past the dead land – these were the components, so to speak, of the frightful silence.

Nowhere was a sign of life to be discerned. The inhabited houses scarcely differed from the others, their doors and windows blocked against the dust, which succeeded anyway in sifting through.

Sometimes, in this floating dust as thick as fog, you could see beside a fence that managed to stay half upright a poor workhorse, its ribs protruding, its head down in the wind, rocking on its legs. Occasionally a small car crossed through this wasteland, so covered with dust you couldn't see its colour, its windows rolled up tight, its lights on in broad daylight, sputtering along toward Horizon.

Like everyone else, Sam Lee Wong hoped for rain. A hundred times a day he would stand in his doorway looking for a clearing in the dust-coloured sky.

The station had closed down, for there were no passengers. Jim Farrell, luckily for him, had managed to find a spot for himself somewhere in northern Saskatchewan where things were a little better. The Saskatchewan Wheat Pool dealer was fired. There was no wheat to buy. Two section supervisors on the railway, regulars in the Chinese café, were laid off as well. Pete Finlinson stayed, but he was possessed again by his savagery and went back to his lonely meals and his endless solitaire, his cat on the table sole witness to his game. The young had left for the cities in search of jobs. The high-backed booths were almost always empty now. Even the bacon smell that had so long pervaded the place began to fade. It gave way to the stronger smell of grasses burnt by the wind and the smell of the earth itself, rasping, catching you by the throat.

In Sam Lee Wong's place things were almost as dreary as in the first days after his arrival in Horizon. At long intervals someone covered with the dust of the land would come in and quickly shut the door behind him. It would be an agronomist, one of the experts sent by the government to see if something couldn't be done for the population; or, very rarely, a frightened travelling salesman who had ventured too far into the dust storm to turn back, and had no choice but to go on to the next village.

With these exceptions Sam Lee Wong saw no one but Smouillya, with whom he spent hours chatting, the Basque straddling a chair – at least you didn't have to mind your manners anymore – and recounting once again from the very start the shaggy tale of his life and hardships. In those days it was drought that had brought him ill-fortune. Now this drought brought it back in force. Across the years misfortune was shaking hands with itself – the eternal repetition of things. Smouillya saw in this a fate that in a way absolved him of his personal failure, a fraternal fate that put everyone on the same footing. You might even get the impression at times that Smouillya was reassured by this monstrous calamity.

Meantime Sam Lee Wong would stare, dazed, at Jim Farrell's favourite chair and imagine him still missing his Margot, whatever he might say; or at Pete Finlinson's, and he would see again the big head with its blond hair; or, longer still, he would stare across at the high-backed booths. Then with a sigh, he would look down between his feet at the linoleum, paid for by instalments after a public health inspector had lectured him on the virtues of cleanliness. Alas! The linoleum was not quite his yet, but already showed signs of wear, especially in front of the counter, and still more at Finlinson's place, for as he told his tales of Iceland he had a habit of scraping the floor with his hobnailed boots.

At times it happened then that Sam Lee Wong, who had after all seen a few things in his day, allowed a shade of astonishment to appear in his expression.

Had he grown much older? It was hard to say. He had

looked ageless even on his arrival. Since then he had grown very thin, quite dried-out, even skinny, but this had happened so slowly that no one remembered how he had looked before: slightly plump. With the years he had acquired a trembling chin, soft and receding, especially when he sank into one of his reveries, his eyes gazing out toward the hills, now barely visible behind the storm and its dark snow.

Once so polite, he was now so altered that he no longer listened to the tireless drone of Smouillya's voice. Smouillya's sight had grown bad, so he didn't notice. To him the absent-minded silence of the Son of the Celestial Empire passed for the profound and smiling attentiveness of other days.

The old man took to leaving late, announcing like a regular whether or not he'd be there for his meals next day.

Sam Lee Wong, behind him, would stand in the doorway for a moment, searching as usual for the profile of the hills.

He had seen many droughts in his time. The memories of them went back as far as his vaguest recollections. His whole life seemed to have been one long drought, apart from a few moments of communication with others. And yet one got over it. People managed to get over it. Standing there in his doorway before going to bed, he waited a long time. In the moonlight, when the wind dropped a little, the hills would reappear, just long enough to give you a glimpse and then another.

The winter was a rough one. The horizon, freed of its dust clouds, grew precise and hard, a cutting edge, and the cold was pitiless as the dry season had been.

Smouillya, with a relapse of his old bronchitis, was unable to leave his cabin for weeks on end. When he emerged he was no more than a string of bones wrapped in sweater after sweater, the whole parcel racked by an incessant wheeze. As soon as it let up for an instant he would go back to his refrain:

money was bound to arrive any day now; he'd come into a heritage over there. With that in his pocket, after his debts, he'd get the heck out of this wretched country.

On these winter nights the contour of the hills beneath the snow was sweet to see. It seemed they were ancient hills linked to the earth's most distant past. Under the stars, their round heads capped in white, they evoked for Sam Lee Wong a notion of infinite old age, a past profound and unmarked, an anchor post at last for this errant life.

He asked Smouillya, then, if he had remembered to send off the monthly payment for his return fare in the coffin. Smouillya grunted that it had been done, for what it was worth, and to the Son of the Celestial Empire that wasn' much.

He went off puffing like a forge, his woollens clutched with both hands across his chest.

Sam Lee Wong returned to his contemplation of the distant hills. Shrivelled, hunched, half frozen, watching motionless from his doorway, he himself took on the form of all things conquered and worn by time.

VII

ut the final blow was not dealt by four years of drought. He
as built to resist that, shrunken to the very limit, needing
ttle food – and as for other wants, had he ever had any? No,
hat dealt the final blow was sudden prosperity.

It fell almost like a catastrophe on the impoverished land,
hich from one day to the next was found to be rich in oil,
ow in one spot, an hour later in another, and finally almost
verywhere for thirty, forty miles around.

As soon as the track was reopened geologists and prospec-
rs came in by the trainload. Then a drilling team, that found
odging anywhere it could in the little village houses. The
mallest room rented for exorbitant prices, even a bed in a
orner. Soon there were secretaries arriving. The station
ummed with constant activity. The bank set up temporary
usiness in a cabin long deserted, while its future home grew
p alongside with great glass panels. The village began to
ook a little as it had in its first days of growth, in the pioneer
mes, but more agitated, more feverish.

For example, take the old spinster on the switchboard,
manda Lecouvreur! Up to now nobody had had an easier

time of it: a call here, a call there…and in the meantime she'd get on with her knitting, warm up her soup, doze a little and, on the really dead days, ring up one of the distant farms to ask, "Anything new out your way?" But now her board was lit up like a Christmas tree. People wanting Regina, Moose Jaw, Swift Current. In ten minutes they wanted more lines than she used to hook up in a whole year. The telephone company, pushed by the oil company, pushed in its turn by Regina, threatened to replace Amanda with someone more efficient.

From a placid old maid she turned brusque, irritable, nervous, and perhaps a little more efficient, with no time for news of people's health or personal affairs, tending only and strictly to business. She could no longer see the human being behind the flashing lights, behind all these voices, familiar or new, that jostled each other in her earphone. But as she was paid a commission on long-distance calls, she made a fortune.

For a few months Sam Lee Wong also picked up a share of the profits raining on the village. The café was never empty. He had built up a reasonable clientele that accepted without too much grumbling what he had to offer: fresh eggs when he'd just bought them, less fresh a little later. But now at the same table they'd order one steak medium, one rare and another medium rare. Sam Lee Wong would go off running, his eyes staring inward so as to engrave the order on his memory; and he might even have managed, but as he passed another table someone would snap his fingers, shouting, "Hey, Charlie! Coffee over here!"

Why did they go calling him Charlie? That put him off his stride for good and all.

And somebody else wanted ice water. Charlie had good cold water, with no bad taste to it, out behind in his well. But it took five minutes to let the bucket down and bring it up full. Meanwhile the steaks were all done the same.

"Hey! I wanted this rare!"

"We're in a rush," they'd say, almost all of them.

"What about that ice cream? Is it gonna be here today?"

Some of them dared to call him back to give a lick of the rag to a table with a little grease on it. Others wanted a "clean" fork.

One day Sam Lee Wong was seen to give up, to do a thing that was completely out of character. He stopped running, remained stock still, took his head in his hands and stared ahead vacantly as if trying to summon up something of his own, an idea, an image, that would reestablish contact between himself and his own reality. He remained thus, frozen in his tracks, quite absent, most disconcerting in the midst of people with not a minute to spare. Then he again became the man they had known since business had picked up: a conscientious Chinaman, a little absent-minded, no longer smiling, even at times daring to raise his voice: "You not satisfied? There a door!" But it should be added that he had heard this phrase a thousand times from Smouillya and had ended by making it his own, not really noticing.

That's how things stood when the mobile kitchen arrived in Horizon, all finished in chrome and aluminum, with hot and cold water and even a refrigerator. The company also moved in trailer sleepers.

Then one day at noon a young woman, a stranger, came and ordered a meal which she never touched. Instead of eating she wrote in a little notebook. Sam Lee Wong hovered some distance away from her, wanting to ask why she didn't eat but not daring. Never had he been subjected to such an indignity. Finally the young person got up. She paid for the meal she had not touched and left without a word. Was she from the Health Department? Was she making a report?

85

In any case, the inspector came back for a visit shortly after. He had never been very severe in his objections in the past.

Sam Lee Wong received him humbly but without too much apprehension. Instinctively he put on his worst English: "You make trip. . .good?"

The inspector pushed past Sam Lee Wong. He went about running his finger along the underside of tables, where people had stuck their used gum, and then along the counter, where it came up greasy.

"Not much time clean lately," Sam Lee Wong apologized. "All the time rush, rush, rush!"

Frowning, the inspector turned to the enclosure at the back. He eyed the contents of a saucepan, tasted a blackish soup, made a face. . . .

A greasy curtain separated this nook, which was the kitchen, from another smaller one. Not standing on ceremony, the inspector lifted it up and peered inside the smaller nook. A few clothes were hanging on nails in the wall. A tiny window, its panes patched with bits of paper, let in a faint gleam of light through its thick coat of grease. The inspector bent down to look under the poor cot, picked up a few rolls of dusty lint and examined the grubby bed with its one grey blanket, turning his nose away as if to inhale as little as possible.

Anxious at the turn the visit was taking, Sam Lee Wong promised a major housecleaning no later than tomorrow.

"Me buy soap very strong and all scrub."

The inspector was still not speaking, except with his eyes and lips which expressed strong disapproval. Finally, asking Sam Lee Wong to sit down for the bad news, he told him the following: unless he refinished the whole place, the mouldy floor, the rotting kitchen, the greasy partitions – in fact the whole works – he would have his restaurant permit cancelled.

Sam Lee Wong was still not upset. After all, he'd been lectured more than once about cleanliness and then they'd let him alone. Yet it was true that today for the first time the inspector had bothered to look in his cooking pots and under the bed. And it just happened, as if on purpose, that on that morning, feeling a little discouraged, Sam Lee Wong had neglected to draw the blanket up over his cot. When it was pulled tight it hung to the floor and hid the dust and lint beneath the bed. He imagined that his misfortune had something to do with this tiny oversight and hastened to make his bed up properly. Then he closed his restaurant, hanging a sign on the door written in Smouillya's fine hand: "Gone on serious business. Back in a few hours."

He went off with short, mincing steps, unused to walking and a little dazzled at finding himself outside in broad daylight – he who for years had barely stuck his nose past his own doorway. And so he was astounded by the changes that had taken place in the village without his noticing. Derricks rose up everywhere on the surrounding plain. Men, black with oil from head to foot, were busy around the drilling rigs. It seemed to him that before, in the sun and wind, with the ripe grain waving in harvest time, the landscape had been a happier one. He remembered the endless fields of wheat and seemed to discover that they had been woven into his life, like the gentle hills of his other memory which still returned at times. Then he became conscious, with a feeling of distress, that in a certain way he had been happy surrounded by the wide, pure spaces of his adopted land but that, like most men, he had allowed his happiness to pass without recognition. Perhaps you had to lose it to know that it had been happiness.

At first he met no one he knew, no one that knew him. Still, a few might have recognized him if they had been able to imagine him out walking in broad daylight like anyone else.

Gradually Sam Lee Wong was filled with a great melancholy and gentle affection for things as they had been, the silent little village to which he had been carried by a memory of hills he might have seen at his life's beginnings; and the people of his first days here and their cordiality!

At least the warm dust blowing around him was the same as then. He made his way to his landlord's house. Each month he had faithfully mailed the amount of his rent, first ten, then fifteen, then suddenly, of late, twenty-five dollars.

He spoke at first, and with a certain self-assurance, of the improvements the Health Department wanted, saying he was willing to assume a part of the cost if the owner – who would have a better property afterwards – would pay his share.

The owner listened in silence, without looking at him, embarrassed. Well, he explained at last, the company had just offered him three thousand dollars for the land where the café stood. The shack was to be torn down. It was a good thing Sam Lee Wong had come along. It saved him the trouble of going into town to tell him about the deal, which was almost closed. He was sorry, but maybe Sam Lee Wong could find another spot, though the little land remaining along the main street had gone sky-high. He was sorry, really sorry! And yet, who could tell? Perhaps it was for the best! Sometimes in life you'd get in a rut and never see it was for your own good to get out of it. Anyway, he wished Sam Lee Wong the best of luck. . .and, oh, by the way, did Sam think he could get out of the place a bit before the three months' notice was up? He'd be paid the difference. . . .

Sam Lee Wong went home so stunned that he didn't even notice several people who this time seemed to recognize him, astonished as they were. "What! Is he still around? It's been years since anybody laid eyes on him!" That's what they seemed to think. It had taken this little daytime excursion of his to remind people of the Chinaman's presence in Horizon.

It was recess and children were playing, just as they had the day he arrived. And what was getting into them now, all of a sudden? They ran up and trapped Sam Lee Wong inside their ring, chanting: "Chinky, chinky Chinaman!" Sam Lee Wong did his best to get in the spirit of the joke. Could he be just arriving in Horizon today? For a moment everything swam inside his head. He'd have to go back where he'd been a moment ago and announce his intention of renting the abandoned granary. He remembered that he had to buy some strong soap. Then he searched his pockets for candies to appease the children. He found only bits of paper he had used as reminders when he was learning by heart the phrases he'd need that day, the kind that would please his customers. "It's a fine day today." Or "spring's coming!" Little by little he recaptured the memory of years gone by, of time irrevocable, and his gaze, like a cry for help, went searching at the plain's end for the gentle, undulating line of the ancient hills.

For a time he was stirred by a desire to fight back. But how to go about it? Write to the Sons of the Orient Aid Society? His dealings with the society had been wound up long ago – ever since he had paid back his debt. If he started writing now the society wouldn't even remember him, and they'd be quite right to ask, "Who's this Sam Lee Wong, asking for money?" Or, if they did remember, they could rightly say, "What! He wants more money now? What a nerve!"

How much would he need? Sam Lee Wong tried to calculate. He thought of the price the owner was getting for the land alone, and reckoned that a modern restaurant would cost as much again, and then he lost his way. He wasn't used to juggling such amounts.

Maybe, he thought, if Sam Lee Wong could arrive nowadays, with Horizon prosperous, but young and enterprising as he had been then, maybe he'd do a big business. That other Sam Lee Wong would know how to go about it. The restaurant would have neon lights, a ventilation hood, even an inside toilet, and perhaps two or three rooms on the first floor up, for company presidents. Fine rooms, with a washbowl in every one. Real style! He dreamed awhile about that younger Sam Lee Wong, saw him grappling with the complications of life today, while he stayed on the sidelines, a spectator, overwhelmed.

For he couldn't make up his mind whether to write to the society. To write, "It's me again, Sam Lee Wong. I need a loan."

"What!" the society would answer. "You had your chance, Sam Lee Wong!"

"That's right," said Sam Lee Wong, bowing his head. "I had my chance."

He simply couldn't see himself rejoining the lineup – which he imagined as having been continuous all these years – from the ship's deck to the most forsaken outposts of this space-rich land. He couldn't see himself stealing the place that belonged to someone else, someone such as he had been – in fact, another Sam Lee Wong.

VIII

There was no one but Smouillya to notice how this skinny Sam Lee Wong was wasting away, sickly from thinking and insomnia, eating less and less, yet never losing his smile. But it was a smile left behind by his gentle humour in retreat, as the sea leaves its mark upon the sand.

During the drought Smouillya had not felt too unhappy, for everyone in those days was more or less in the same boat. But now that people went riding around in Buicks, going to the bank once a day, planning trips to Texas, how could he help feeling like the only one of his kind! Himself abandoned, Smouillya began to realize what might be in store for Sam Lee Wong. He succeeded in getting him to talk. He discovered the impossible tangle of difficulties in which the Chinaman was struggling. Filled with indignation and the energy it gave his feeble body, he went off at once down the main street to alert people to the news, stopping this one and that one, shouting at each of them. "Listen, we've got to do something for Sam Lee Wong, damn it! He's been living in this town twenty-five years. He's one of us, we can't just let him go to pot without doing something for him. Come on, have a heart, let's do something together for Sam Lee Wong!"

At first when they saw old Smouillya veering toward them, people tried to dodge him, thinking, Oh oh! Here he comes! He's good for half an hour, let's get going! But Smouillya would grab them by the sleeve or simply bar the way. And talk and talk and talk! In the whine of the hot wind he put his whole talent into the wretched story, sputtering in the faces of his listeners who would back off as he advanced, keeping the distance about the same. All the while Smouillya's eyes, filled with a surprising eloquence, begged for attention as they had never done. But it was a waste of time. Nobody understood him. He tried English. If anything, that was worse. Out of politeness or laziness a few people pretended to understand, but Smouillya knew from their eyes that they did nothing of the sort, and he was taken by a kind of despair.

Where could he go? Who would listen to him? Suddenly he saw the light and dashed to the telephone company's switchboard. In the days when he'd been a good-looking fellow and people put up with his speech defect, he had paid court to Miss Lecouvreur, who had, it was not impossible to believe, been in love with him. He turned up in front of her and shouted over the buzzing of her board: "Amanda! Amanda! Listen with the heart you used to have. For God's sake, listen to me. Hear what's happened to Lee Wong!"

Amanda, her head gripped by her earphones, looking like a traveller about to leave, an aviator or a deep-sea diver, frowned, saying to herself, If I listen to him, Lord knows what I'm getting into. He'll still be here this time tomorrow. But hooked by who knows what sudden curiosity she switched everything off and removed her earphones.

"All right, make it fast. It could cost me my job, you know, listening to you."

Then, perhaps feeling a little remorse, Amanda realized that when she paid complete attention she could grasp a word of his gibberish here and there. Perhaps the old man was making a special effort to be understood today. Amanda, reading his lips, watching his eyes – their expression filled in the meaning – began to get the thread of this irregular torrent of language. She finally understood that it was about Sam Lee Wong and that he had to leave, but she got the rest all wrong. She understood that Sam was retiring from business to go back to China. And she said, "Fine, just leave it to me. I'll look after the whole thing, don't worry." And she went back inside her earphone.

She had already decided that if Sam Lee Wong was leaving they certainly couldn't let him go without giving him a party. In the old days, when Amanda's life had been monotonous, there'd been no one like her for organizing parties. Arrival parties, going-away parties; paper weddings, tin weddings, gold and silver weddings and jubilees of every kind.

Now a little of the old fever overtook her again. For a few minutes she let the executives in Calgary and Moose Jaw and Swift Current languish at their phones while she busied herself calling as many people as possible in the village and on the farms.

As she went on explaining her plan for a party in Sam Lee Wong's honour, the plan grew bigger and bigger and she herself was caught up in the game.

"It's almost twenty-five years," she'd say, "that Sam Lee Wong's been living here among us. You could say he's an early bird, an old-timer. Now, are we going to let an old-timer leave without getting back a taste of the good old days? For he was part of those days!"

The good old days! Now that they were rich, people thought nostalgically of the past. Amanda had them all on the string when she talked that way. Neighbourliness, loyalty, fidelity to the good old days! This emotion, revived, turned to Sam Lee Wong's benefit. He was leaving! You couldn't let him go without marking your regret.

At once a flock of good-wills were on the wing. Mrs. Connoly would take care of the cakes and cookies, Madame Toutant would do the turkey. A committee of honour was formed. They reserved the town hall for the evening of the second Saturday in November. And in the meantime, shhhhh! not a word that could spoil Sam Lee Wong's surprise. One of the committee ladies, thinking of Sam Lee Wong's origins, had the idea of decorating the hall with Chinese lanterns. Adopted unanimously! Making the lanterns was left to the schoolteacher, who found a pattern in the *Encyclopedia Britannica*. She had her pupils cut them out in quantity from brightly coloured paper. The class was overjoyed. The children clipped and assembled and glued the paper after the model. The teacher took the opportunity of saying a few things about China, a great country that produced much rice and many floods, and told them all about mandarins and coolies, and how the latter pulled the former in rickshaws.

The hardest thing was to keep the project from getting out of hand, as the village hadn't had a going-away party for a long time. Why not hire a little square-dance group like in the old days? Done. They found a fiddler and a caller unequalled for getting the sets on their feet. They asked the priest to say a few words. Baptists, Catholics, Lutherans, Swedes, Finns, Russians, French – they all found it exciting to catch the spirit of the party. In the first place, it had one most original aspect: giving a party for an Oriental was somehow a sign of rare cosmopolitanism, and it pushed back

Horizon's frontiers considerably. And then, it was for Sam Lee Wong, who had gone through the good and bad years with them – a whole quarter-century. That was really something in a province like Saskatchewan which itself had barely more years than that to its credit.

But what should they give the café owner as a going-away present? The argument was heated. If only they had listened to the sensible voices who favoured a sum of money! Alas, it was the eternal gold watch that prevailed. With a gold chain as well, the whole works! They ordered it from a jeweller in Moose Jaw. Sam Lee Wong's name was to be engraved on it.

Then they started hanging the lanterns in the hall. They looked simply splendid. Old Smouillya held his tongue the whole time, though with difficulty, for he watched Sam Lee Wong sink ever deeper in his distress and could hardly resist the temptation to reveal the joys that awaited him.

IX

The autumn passed quickly. That Saturday it already felt like winter. In Sam Lee Wong's rickety cabin the nails in the walls creaked with the dry cold. He was all alone at one of his little tables; from time to time he looked up and smiled vaguely as if following with his gaze someone who had just come in and gone to sit at the other side of the room. In his boredom he nearly began to talk aloud to these imaginary customers, all phantoms from the past. In fact, Sam Lee Wong had an excellent memory. In a sense he had not forgotten a single person who had come to his restaurant, even if it were only to buy a package of cigarettes; but of course it was with his regulars that he was having his imaginary conversation. He invoked those who had been meticulous and polite, those who said thank you when their soup came – nothing much, but Sam Lee Wong remembered it – and those who carved at his tables with their penknives. He thought of them all with almost equal regret. Suddenly the door opened on the bitter cold and Smouillya appeared, unrecognizable, washed, shaven and combed. He headed for the nook at the back and

Sam Lee Wong's good suit, which he brought out to him, saying: "Come on, get into your Sunday suit. It's a special night!"

Sam Lee Wong thought Smouillya was playing a joke, and he was so pleased to see him happy that he did as he was asked. He put on the suit, and it hung so loose that the two of them burst out laughing, partly in nervousness and partly because it was funny, for Sam Lee Wong had to take very short steps in order not to lose his pants. Smouillya took care of that with a piece of binder-twine, and away they went, walking slowly because of the flapping pants, on snow that squeaked with little, soft cries under their feet. It was a night for a feast. The stars shone brightly, and so did the windows of the distant town hall. Sam Lee Wong saw nothing surprising in that, nor in being dragged thither by Smouillya, who couldn't stop laughing. There was a touch of festivity in the air, and in Sam Lee Wong's heart a contentment that corresponded a little to it. For yesterday he had glimpsed a kind of solution. Why not, in fact, make way for a young and enterprising Chinese like the Sam Lee Wong of former times, while he himself would become a laundryman? With all these newly rich in Horizon there'd be no lack of fine shirts to wash and iron by hand. And if he'd learned before to be a restaurant-keeper, why couldn't he learn the laundry business now? All in all, it was less complicated than the other.

His relief was so great that he felt like telling Smouillya. But it was Smouillya's turn, in his joy at having a surprise for Sam Lee Wong, to listen to no one, still less to poor Sam Lee Wong trotting along at his side.

In single file they entered the hall with its splendour of lanterns and its crowd of happy faces. There was a burst of applause. Sam Lee Wong smiled to the right, then to the left, at all these people who (wasn't it odd?) seemed to be looking at him with the same warm expression; but it must be for Smouillya. Then a catchy tune was struck up, and at the same time everyone gathered around him to sing, "For he's a jolly good fellow, for he's a jolly good fellow. . . ." And then more applause! People laughed when they saw Sam Lee Wong's expression and gave him friendly slaps on the shoulder, and he too began to laugh a little, though a touch of anxiety showed in his eyes.

Then Amanda came to take his hand and lead him up on the platform where the dignitaries were already seated. And there was Sam Lee Wong sitting between the priest and the mayor, exposed to the gaze of all, trying at least to hide his feet under the chair, for he had changed everything but his shoes.

The mayor stood up. He spoke for rather a long time about someone who had arrived in Horizon twenty-five years ago when the village, as they must remember, was just a few houses; and how he had worked hard with the others to make it the fine and prosperous little town it was today. A man who had laid his stone in the building and put his shoulder to the wheel! When he returned to the land of his birth, in honourable retirement from business, he could be sure that he had left behind a lasting memory.

Applause! Sam Lee Wong was just about to start clapping with the others but held back, pierced by a mysterious apprehension. The priest in his turn made a speech, and again the subject was honourable retirement and a memory that would never fade away.

Then a little girl in a white dress, her hair in a bow, curtsied in front of Sam Lee Wong and laid in his hands a slim box wrapped in tissue paper. From the dignitaries' looks he saw that he was supposed to open the little package. Sam Lee Wong stared long at the gold watch. He passed it to the mayor, who passed it to the priest, who gave it back to Sam Lee Wong. Then each of them turned to shake his hand, and everybody was clapping him on the back and saying, "Have a good trip, Sam Lee Wong! Happy retirement!"

Going home alone through the frozen night, abandoned even by Smouillya who had taken a drop and felt unwell, alone under the sky-vault so busy with stars that it made one think of the immeasurable exile of man on earth, Sam Lee Wong began to understand more or less clearly what was happening to him. He would have to leave. For he was the one they'd been saying goodbye to. It was he who had been congratulated by the mayor, who had been praised to the skies by the priest. What could he do here after all that? His eyes looked down at the earth and seemed to have dulled for all time.

For though he had lived apart from the village he had occasionally seen just this series of circumstances: someone would be treated like a king and almost immediately he'd be taking a train; he'd go away so far that no one would ever hear of him again. It must be the unwritten law of these parts. As soon as a whole village started to like someone publicly, that person had no choice but to be on his way.

On his way! Of course Sam Lee Wong had welcomed the notion, but only as a terminal adventure. When his short life here below was ended. When the time had come to go, in his coffin, to join his ancestors. Apart from them, who would care two cents whether he ever returned to great, swarming China? Perhaps even they, the ancestors, in their leaden slumber had ended by forgetting their lost child!

X

Through these slight hills, not really far from the village, that
had attracted Sam Lee Wong from a much greater distance
and then drawn him to his doorstep in contemplation almost
every day, he had never once managed to travel as a simple
sightseer. And here he was in the midst of them, sitting snugly
in the train, his old suitcase beside him on the seat and, on
the floor, a big parcel tied with cord.

A few of his old customers who had come to say goodbye
at the station were surprised to see him take the eastbound
train to go to China. Wouldn't it have been shorter to go back
the way he had come, by Vancouver and the Pacific Ocean?
But, they speculated, maybe Sam Lee Wong had finally
decided to have a look around before leaving the country.

As long as he remained visible to his friends (who were
stamping in the snow to keep warm, shouting through thick
clouds of frosty breath, "Happy landings, Charlie! . . .") Sam
Lee Wong had almost succeeded in getting into the high
spirits of his send-off. Then he caught himself nodding and
smiling at the fences and fields that had begun to slide past

100

his window, but soon the old, familiar weariness took the place of nods and smiles and settled in again on his face. Now the train was labouring up the slope that led to the isolated little chain of hills. Sam Lee Wong moved closer to the window to at last have a good look at these cherished hills that had cast their spell over his whole life. But they no longer evoked or connected up with his childhood hills, which had somehow dissolved into these.

Inscribed on the horizon, he saw a slow-moving undulation, arrested and held for all time, as if (you might imagine) it were meant to rock asleep forever the immemorial distress of man. The hills were covered with snow. It rounded off their already rounded heads with their attitude of patience, of listening to some long story whispered up from the valleys' hollow. On the protected side, small trees bore brown and shrivelled leaves upon their branches, still trembling as if with a vestige of life in the breathing air. Sam Lee Wong saw no houses or outbuildings of any kind. Strange that a railway was there to carry you through such a wild and desolate scene.

In fact, it cut through the hills at the narrowest point, with a branch line that ran down as fast as it could to join the main track. The branch, and a whistle stop, had been built in former years to serve a few fine ranches located in the hills. Of these practically no trace remained. The train rushed through the whistle stop. A little later it emerged from the hills onto a plain so amazingly like the one he had left that Sam Lee Wong sat blinking, as if he couldn't believe his eyes. The same flat immensity. The same faint, dotted line of fence posts barely poking out of the snow, like the tracks of an animal in a straight line across the stretch of white. Human life reappeared in frail clusters of houses, then in bare villages. Sam Lee Wong scrutinized from afar the profile of each. He was on the lookout for one that would impress him.

He hoped for a village that would be big enough but not too big. Just enough to keep a café going. He had learned from the conductor that the first five or six villages on this side of the hills had no restaurant, and that two of them might just fill the bill for a café-keeper, if he wasn't fussy, of course.

Well, the train was slowing down just as it entered one of the villages that combined the qualities required. Sam Lee Wong could make out a snow-covered main street, little wooden houses on just one side of it, grain elevators – in short, a landscape as familiar as his memory of Horizon the day that he arrived. . . . But that had been on a sunny September day, and now the wind was whipping by in icy gusts. Never mind! Sam Lee Wong hastened to lug his suitcase and his big parcel to the steps of the carriage. He'd have to hurry. The train tarried no more than a minute or two at these almost lifeless whistle stops. Sam Lee Wong barely managed to drag his belongings down to the platform when the conductor ran out from the next car, waving his arms in protest, shouting: "You not get off here. Ticket good yet!"

From the platform, to reassure this kind man who seemed concerned about him, Sam Lee Wong shouted back: "Me not wish go further. Here all right! Very all right!"

The conductor threw up his arms as if to say, What can you do. . . for human beings! Already the train was picking up speed. It left behind the frail silhouette encumbered by its packages. A gust of wind caught Sam Lee Wong's grey scarf and wrapped it around his face, forcing him to grope for a few steps. At last he reached the station, set down his things and pulled away the scarf, which had half-blocked his vision. He found that his gaze was probing implacable and howling distances. He clambered over a high bank of snow ploughed up at the edge of the main street. He reached the trodden path that served as a sidewalk. There he stopped to empty snow from one felt boot. Then he went off in search of space to rent. That, it seemed, would not be hard to find, for a good part of the village was abandoned. Its only luxury, lying beyond its twenty-odd houses and set back a little in the fields, was a long hut with a corrugated tin roof: the curling rink. A good sign, that. It meant customers at night, after the game! And in fact that same evening some villagers going home from curling saw a light in the former barn that had been moved into the village to provide an office for the itinerant agronomist. One said, "Hey, that won't be bad, sandwich and coffee after the games!"

In the light of a naked bulb hanging by its cord from the ceiling they could see an old man with slanted eyes, his apron on, cleaning, tidying, like a bird that builds his nest where the world calls him. Some of them had the notion of going in to give him a hand or at least say a word of welcome. The others dragged them off, saying, "Aw, come on, you never know with these Chinks when they get old. Sometimes they get cranky. Let's wait and see, anyhow."

On a fine winter morning a few days later, you could read the following sign drawn in soap on the freshly washed window (less impressive, though, than the one in Horizon):

RESTAURANT SAM LEE WONG
FULL COURSE MEALS
SNACKS
SOFT DRINKS

And in a corner, in smaller letters:

Ice Cream, Soda, Cigars

Sam Lee Wong himself, in his apron, his grey scarf around his neck, stood in the half-open doorway, despite the biting cold, waiting for his first customer. He knew from long experience that an open door was half the battle. Since no one showed up, he had all the time in the world to daydream as he gazed far across the snow-covered plain, blowing on his fingers to keep them warm.

And the miracle was there! From his new threshold he found that he could see as well as previously, but from the other side, the frail outline of the gentle hills imprinted on the winter blue of the horizon.

Before to his left, now on his right, they were still a part of his life. So there was no need to despair. Perhaps his ancestors hadn't quite lost track of their child who had landed. . .where? What was it now, the name of this village? Oh yes! Sweet Clover, Saskatchewan. . . .

He concentrated. He engraved the name in his mind with care, with diligence, as if it were a piece of information he must make known somewhere, if he were to be found at last.

He lifted his eyes up to the hills. The place he had been walking toward all his life could not be much farther now.

Hoodoo Valley

Hoodoo Valley

The group of Doukhobors newly arrived in Verigin, a prairie hamlet, were living for the time being in the round tents and converted railway cars that had been provided for them: a melancholy encampment on a hostile terrain invested by marshes, mosquitoes and, worse still, every evening, by boredom. Then, gathered like an immense family around a fire of branches, you could hear them intoning, all with the same low-pitched, afflicted voice, some song of their people.

No Doukhobor was ready to say it right out loud, but they were desolate.

"It's nothing like our Humid Mountains."

"Oh, no! Far it is from our green Caucasus!"

From the very start the plain had set about rebuffing them with its flat immensity, naked under the sky, this endless space, this too-vast exaggeration of a land where in winter, they said, it was cold enough to freeze your breath in your throat, and in summer hot enough to put an end to your days. And the people here, the ones who'd been living in this soli-

...while, what strange ones they were! Eaters of meat and other forbidden foods, they squabbled among themselves as if life wasn't hard enough already; or, carried away by a different madness, they'd dance till the tavern tables jumped. They couldn't be Christians, these folk who used alcohol and tobacco and never seemed to tire of spatting viciously among themselves.

The Doukhobor women, their blond hair carefully hidden under kerchiefs doubled to a point, had perhaps less time for boredom than their men. They cooked over little piles of embers, did the washing, laid it to dry on the grass, and went off across the naked plain, sometimes quite a distance, searching for bits of wood to burn. But their husbands, these great stalwarts, upright as oaks, with heavy moustaches, their blue eyes childlike and astonished, had all the leisure they needed for sighing and lamenting.

Their leaders, Streliov, Zibinov and Strekov, went out every day with their guide McPherson, the settlement agent, sometimes to the north, sometimes to the south, in search of land for their community. Up to now they had nowhere found a concession that in their eyes combined the qualities they obscurely felt would suit them.

The man McPherson, an ambitious and enterprising little Scot, had wagered that he'd settle his Doukhobors in no time, intending to use their success on Canadian soil as a stepping stone to promotion in his career.

The women, the children, the old men, would surround the three leaders on their return to the encampment and ask: "What did you see today, Zibinov, Streliov, Strekov?"

And these three, the men in whom they had placed their confidence, would reply: "Just the flat land. The same as here."

"And that was all?"

"Just prairie, I tell you. Nothing but prairie."

McPherson was fuming. What else did they expect to find here in the flattest stretch of all Canada?

A strange folk, gentle, dreaming, with only one foot in this world; but in their refusal, their disillusion, they had a tenacity that could outlast the most energetic. The people of the village, a handful of neighbours, immigrants themselves but resigned with good grace to their new land, began to grow impatient with these long-faced Doukhobors whose incessant plaintive songs reached them night after night in their scattered shacks. As if singing could change the prairie! It had heard other sighs, seen other regrets, this plain of exile and homesickness. In the end it always brought people around. Others, many others, had been through the same thing. The Doukhobors too would have to give in.

They didn't want to break up or settle in small groups as others did. That would have solved many problems, for the good land was by no means all in one place. Most often it was a patchwork created by ancient alluvia or waterways. But they absolutely refused to separate. They insisted on settling in a single region, old and young, grandchildren and grandparents together, along with nephews, cousins and friends – in short, the whole lost folk in one place.

So they sought a big stretch of arable land. At some distance from the camp such tracts of land were still to be found. McPherson took Strekov, Streliov and Zibinov to see them, across miles and miles of silent plain, often serene and inviting under the high, clear sky. Where the road stopped the wagon made its own trail through the grasses. In this way they'd seen a good part of the countryside: sandy, desert-like spaces overrun by the wind; others with a stubby growth like wire twisted and rolled together; others made almost livable by pretty groups of trees that showed from afar the presence of water. Nowhere did the Doukhobor leaders consent to stop.

"Nyet, nyet."

Here the country seemed too wild, too isolated; there they would spy tents or trappers' huts and suddenly were unwilling to have neighbours.

"Nyet, nyet!"

They shook their heads. Their eyes, blue and candid, wide with astonishment, always expressed the same tenacious estrangement.

And this had been going on for weeks.

The women were constantly on the lookout for the party's return.

"Come now, you must have seen something today that would suit us!"

"Nyet. We saw nothing but the flat land. Always the same."

They could find no other way to express their disappointment. Before they left the Caucasus, someone must have told them a very fancy story to attract them to the Canadian West, and they'd swallowed it whole. They always ended up singing their songs of lamentation. At such times the gentle landscape they had left behind, the land of acacias, of lemon trees and tender grass, came to life again behind their closed eyelids. For each new evil chases out the last; having forgotten the persecutions that had forced them to leave their native soil, their hearts retained nothing of it but the most tender recollections.

Oh, what nostalgia!

By now even the women were almost all infected by it.

This wretched plain all around! (At times you could see one of them stoop to pick up a pebble and hurl it violently as if to strike the immense countryside and take vengeance on its numb expanse.)

"What did you see today, Streliov?" asked Makaroff, the oldest and wisest, who thought the time had come to make the best of a bad job. Life wasn't so long, he often said. If we have to use up so much of it regretting the past, what's left for doing what's still to be done?

And Streliov, the oldest of the three leaders, a solid man with all the strength of his thirty years, began to sigh like a stripling.

"The same thing as here, Grandfather. The naked plain, always. And always, it seems, the same cruel indifference."

The old man drew nearer to poke the fire.

"I remember when I was young and we'd just been exiled to the Caucasus, life didn't seem so easy there either at the start. Did you say 'indifference,' Streliov? Do you have any idea how many trees – lemon trees and cherry trees and acacias – we had to plant there for every one that lived? Do you know that, Streliov?"

The immigrants, seated in a circle in the growing dark, were suddenly as struck by his words as they had been by their recurrent longing for their lost homeland. At once their eyes turned outward toward the plain which their imagination saw as endless: the mute, the enigmatic land. They did their best to see it covered with little whitewashed houses, with pens for the chickens, vegetable gardens, fences, milk pails upside down on the fence posts, busy comings and goings, and even their seesaw wells like the ones at home in the Caucasus, punctuating the prairie with the long strokes of their lever poles drawn dark against the sky. For awhile they were all comforted by the vision of the tremendous work to be redone and they burned with impatience to get started.

"True enough, you know," some of the more realistic women grumbled, "it's more than time we started in some-where. You leaders, go off on your search again. And try to come back with some good news. It's high time to get on with our work."

But others, lulling their babies, held them tight to their breast as if defying the dark plain to steal them away. And suddenly they would begin to weep, doubtless because of some vague perception that the plain would finally take their children, would take thousands of others, would absorb as many lives as there were grains of sand, before this would even show. Still others, a few about to bear children, had an even stronger hatred of the stark land and the giant sky which their eyes probed in terror.

The ones with the most common sense were the very old women, tottering babushkas, come to this country with just enough time left to die and sleep in its foreign soil.

They scolded the younger ones: "What would our holy little father Verigin think, and him in exile in the wilds of Siberia, if he saw you now, downcast and fearful and always snivelling?"

And the others would reply: "Our little father Verigin promised we'd find peace at the end of the world, and harmony, and that in the place we went to we'd be of one heart and mind. Perhaps we didn't understand his orders. Did he really mean us to come to Canada?"

A very angry babushka scolded back: "There's no such thing as a country where we can be of one mind unless we try, each one of us, to make it so. Our little father Verigin promised us a land where they'd let us live in peace according to our ideal of non-violence and free conscience. He didn't promise the grass would be trimmed and the house all built and the bread on the table. Have you all gone mad? Tell me! The old Doukhobors of my time put more heart in their work and whined less. And they'd seen something of cruelty and injustice, before our good Loukeria, in those dark years when

112

they wandered over Russia. What about those who fell under the knout of the Czarist soldiers rather than take arms against their brothers? Did you ever hear that they grumbled? Shame to these Doukhobors around me!"

In the end they prayed together under the great starlit sky. At least the stars were still familiar. Their eyes raised on high, they asked for a light to guide them on their earthly path.

"Little mother, it's not the work we're afraid of. It's the silence here. It's as if God no longer wanted to give us a sign. As if from now on he would be silent forever."

The wrinkled face, furrowed by life, was absorbed in contemplation of the flames.

"It is true. Since we came to Canada he has seldom spoken to us. But he is there, behind all that silence. Just wait, my lambs. Tomorrow, the next day, one day soon, he will surely give us a sign."

II

Forty miles north of the railway a great stretch of grassy plain, formerly pastureland to a herd of buffalo, was still there for the taking. That was the destination of the expedition that set out on a certain July morning.

The heavy wagon lumbered along at the trot – often a slow one – of the four prairie horses, all small but solidly built. Six men were in the party: the three Doukhobor leaders, then McPherson, flanked by his interpreter, James Craig, and the half-breed driver. They had left at dawn accompanied by particularly fervent women's voices raised in song, for after the long evening of prayer everyone had risen with the conviction that this day, at last, would be marked by divine favour.

At first they drove across a plain where a reddish grass waved as far as you could see; then others where a thick growth of weeds rose to the wagon's axles; saline patches harboured the noxious smells of many carcasses of young deer and dead birds; brushwood country, and muskegs where everyone had to get off and help the horses; morose landscapes where there was nothing living but the wind; and, from time to time, fresh little stands of elder trees or poplar. Almost everywhere the plain seemed uninhabited and silent.

Each patch of green in this limitless landscape could be seen for miles around, and this was all that kept the tired beasts going or altered the men's unblinking stare.

Evening was not far off. Still nothing hinted that they might be nearing the former buffalo pasture. McPherson was growing worried. Had they taken the wrong fork at the last faint crossing of the ways?

No path was visible now. They were navigating by guesswork across rocky soil or through virgin grass. The half-breed driver seemed as uncertain as the little horses themselves. Their ears pricked up anxiously from time to time. The leaders, impassive in the back, pretended to ignore these disturbing developments.

Suddenly McPherson exclaimed loudly in vexation. The land was changing without warning. For in fact, on emerging from a gulley of shadows that had hemmed them in for several minutes, they were met by an intense and gleaming light. There a new landscape stood revealed, one of surprising beauty, unsuspected even a moment ago.

It was Hoodoo Valley, so named by the Indians who were frightened of its strangeness and the curious power it had—precisely at this hour of day—over the unstable souls of men.

With an exotic splendour, more reminiscent of the Orient than of the plain with its assortment of quiet shades, it flamed up before them in the floods of copper light the sun spilled over it at this day's end. Countless flowers, pushing up through brambles and tall, sharp-bladed grass, gave off a glow in that light almost not to be borne. Flowers among which not one, so people said, was without its sting, its poison sap, its capacity to wound; but all strangely sumptuous, in umbels of garnet velvet, bunched heads of sombre gold, purple or milky corollas with stiff, smooth leaves shining with their lacquer.

In the distance clouds tinted blazing red enclosed this odd valley, surrounding it as with a chain of hills whose folds held an indefinable attraction. Each one appeared to open into the reddened sky a secret and mysterious passage toward a place where certainty and happiness must reign at last. From one minute to the next, moreover, beneath the constant flaming of the sky, the more distant clouds took on further depth and issued their silent call.

McPherson, almost caught in the spell for a moment, though he'd have been the last to admit it, got hold of himself. He hated this place above all others. He was about to give the order to leave at once when the three leaders, on their feet in the back of the wagon, began encouraging each other excitedly: "Da, da!"

This was the first time McPherson had heard them say yes.

Further words seemed torn from them by their excess of emotion and the infinite joy of being there together, all three unanimous.

"What's that they're saying?" asked McPherson.

The interpreter smiled with some commiseration.

"They want to get off here. They're talking about the Humid Mountains, something about receiving a sign at last. . .and I don't know what-all, it doesn't make much sense. . . ."

As if under a spell, they were barely recognizable, their faces lit up and transformed, their eyes gleaming. With one accord they leapt from the wagon and advanced toward the valley. Stones rolled beneath their feet, a fine dust rose from the earth where they walked, and this alone should have told them of the poverty of the soil; but the Doukhobors paid no attention, their eyes dazzled, advancing in line toward the brilliance the setting sun had managed to extract from an inextricable tangle of thorn and thistle.

They stopped. One raised his arm and pointed to the mass of clouds resting on the sky's edge, forming enchanting hills that rolled back to beyond this world. Another pointed at the long streak of light that wound across the valley like a river of pale waters. The third fervently stared out at the fiery horizon.

"What do they say?"

"That there's all you need here to rejoice the heart of man," the interpreter said. "Mountains in the distance, a river in the grass, a rare kind of peace and birds everywhere."

True enough, for look! The burning air was filled with the presence of birds! Nesting in the serried thickets, calling from bush to bush, then, all at once, with great cries and whirring of wings, bursting into flight; creatures with flaming throats, crested with red or light yellow, thronged into the air. But these were unsociable birds and fled from men: their presence here, like that of the strange flowers, spoke further of the wildness of the place.

"But those aren't mountains yonder," McPherson tried to explain, "and that's no river in the valley. Tell them, Craig, that it's all mirage and trumpery. It's the sun and the time of day that make the cursed valley turn this way at sunset!"

But it was no use. The three Doukhobors had removed their hats as if to salute one of the most moving encounters of their lives. They stayed motionless a long time, their eyes moist, contemplating the landscape and listening to their conquered hearts.

"They know, at least I think they do," the interpreter reported, "that the mountains and rivers aren't real, but they say, 'What's the difference, as long as we can see them? And if the three of us, by God's grace, can see again in this place the mountains and river of our sweet homeland, why should it be any different for our wives and children and old men? Won't they see these things too? And when they've seen them, won't they be reassured, as we are?'"

Then McPherson, forgetting that they couldn't understand him, shouted: "Just scratch that soil! See how poor it is! Look at that confounded brush, it's all that'll grow here. I can give you a hundred times better, a thousand times better! I can give you lovely flat fields where the grass is so tasty your horses'll whinny a mile away. Or if you want I'll find you land that's half woods and a real river running through it. Just a few hours from here, all that's waiting for you!"

But the Doukhobors would hear none of it. Beyond the call of reason now, exiled in elation, assured that they alone understood the world's mystery, they stood there, hat in hand, imagining that they had perhaps been shown an infallible sign of destiny. They took one pace forward and struck up a song of thanksgiving. The song found its way down the valley and echoed back twice, three times. The great, wild birds, and the dry leaves rustling at their passage, seemed shaken with surprise at hearing an old, exalted hymn rolling all the way from ancient Russia.

At last the three men ended their song. McPherson saw that they were weeping. Tears rushed impetuously from their eyes, washing the dust from their cheeks and disappearing in their blond moustaches. They wept without raising a hand to wipe their cheeks, in abandon and confidence, relieved once and for all of the cruelty of expectation.

McPherson waited yet awhile. Soon there would be an end to the fugitive beauty of the place. In a moment now it would be left bare: when the great footlight on the horizon dimmed, perhaps they would see that this was nothing but a wasteland under false, flamboyant colours.

But now the Doukhobors were showing their impatience to be gone. They were in a hurry to bring the good news to the others.

They sat on one side of the wagon, facing the same way. They were looking back when suddenly the valley dimmed into twilight and what was perhaps its true and poignant gloom. But in the shadow there still glowed on their inscrutable faces the flaming sky that their eyes had seen and their souls now bore away.

Garden in the Wind

Garden in the Wind

Farther on, farther still than Codessa – that little Ukrainian capital of sorts in the Canadian North – after you've travelled for hours on an endless dirt road and beyond a wild stretch of plain, you suddenly see signs of what once upon a time tried to be a village. This is the place called Volhyn, in Alberta, and to tell the truth there's almost nothing to it, apart from the immensity and the solitary stroke of the road through it; above, the phone lines hum inexplicably in the air.

To one side of this poor track is an old-fashioned schoolhouse, with its *teacherage*, and beside it, a woodpile; all three abandoned. It's been a long time since the voices of children were heard here, or the bell that called them.

Even more enigmatic in its remoteness, all alone beyond the fields, there is a tiny prayer house, an odd kind of chapel. Barely seven or eight people could find room inside. Yet it was built just like a church and has all the parts: a bit of a porch preceded by three steps, a touch of stained-glass in the narrow slits that serve as windows, and even a little onion-shaped steeple. Nothing could be so strange in this flat expanse of uninhabited land as this reminder of the Orthodox faith.

Inside the prayer house spider webs cover the faces of aged icons. The dust of old bouquets of wild flowers lies where it has lain for years, at the feet of Saint Basil and Saint Vladimir. A madonna with faded features seems worn out by age and thankless labours. Outside, a never-ending moan: the prairie wind blows here like a sea wind, bringing the same unease, ceaselessly curling and whipping at the grasses as it does in water.

It was around the years 1919 and 1920 that this land was, as they say, opened for settlement. At that time a little group of peasants, most of them illiterates, came to these parts with their bundles and their babies, having left their native Volhynia months before. It was the first voyage of their lives, and they had crossed a continent, then the ocean, then most of another continent. Bewildered, they had pushed on with horses still farther across a solitude that grew from day to day, to reach at last, on a day in spring, this long, grassy plain that opened before their eyes like some endless reverie on man and his destiny.

Did they then have the feeling that all roads were wiped out behind them, that they would never come alive out of this extremity? And are they now all dead or disbanded?

Not quite. The road, straight for so long, at last bends slightly. A little aspen grove appears, all trembling with light, its leaves reversed, its branches trimmed to a man's height – the kind that in the West is a sign of an immigrant farm. Then a living house. And in the same moment, flowers. A mass of flaming colours that strike your eye, seize your heart.

So it was that one day, when a strange curiosity – or rather that melancholy, that taste for seeking out and sharing the most utter solitude which often possesses me – guided me along that road, I saw before me, under the enormous sky, against the hostile wind and among the tall grasses, this little garden, fairly bursting with flowers.

In those days I often said to myself: what's the point of this, what's the good of that? Writing was a chore for me. Why bother inventing yet another story – would it be closer to reality than the facts themselves? Who still believes in stories? And in any case, haven't they all been told? That's what I was thinking that day when, toward evening on that road which seemed to lead me nowhere, I saw in the very emptiness of drought and desolation that surge of splendid flowers.

Scarlet poppies with their dark core, others, their warm pink rimmed with a stronger hue, some like fine, white silk rumpled in your hand, offered their delicately pleated faces to the dry wind. How long could they cling to life in this rough wind? Perhaps not a single day. In double ranks lupines on their slender spikes wavered like candle flames in a wind-blown procession. But the delphiniums, now, turned back to the sky its own gaze of indifferent blue. Geraniums in brighter tones, fragile snapdragons, their small throats swollen as if from milk or honey, some flowers tall and haughty, others timid, all pressed close together as if in boundless surprise at being there. Had I ever, until that moment, seen flowers at all? Have I ever truly seen them since? Perhaps only on that deserted road from Volhyn have I been quite penetrated by the mystery of this world called flowers.

Sometimes even now when the vision of that little garden on the edge of the inhabited earth comes back to mind, I think: it was a dream and nothing more!

But then other things come back to mind as well: the face, the smile, the memory of Marta.

Her full name: Maria Marta Yaramko.

At least on her grave, hidden among the tall wild barley and meadow grass, on the wooden cross that barely rises clear, that's what is written, letter after shaky letter, as if by a hand that scarcely knew how to write.

Here then is her story as I discovered it, piece by piece.

II

Early that morning, despite the pain that woke in her body with her own awakening, Marta went out of the low, white-washed house, a white kerchief tied beneath her chin, her apron billowing, to reconnoitre the sprouts in her garden which were barely showing out of their seeds, just pushing into life. For springtime had managed to come once more, that spring which out Volhyn way surely had a longer and harder road to go than in any other corner of the world. The wind on high spoke of it in the heavens, and the lively plants, sowed in other days when Marta had faith and hope, showed themselves still full of health and youth. At her feet she recognized a leaf, so newly emerged from its sheath that it still had the shape of its former casing. With her hand she helped this birth along, brushing away a twig that could hinder it, crushing to dust around it a crumb of earth that could seem mountainous to such a tiny creature. She stood up, within sight of this small, unfolding life, and contemplated the disconcerting size of sky and earth. Why did her garden, started when she was young, still force her to take care of it? Why, in her old age, so much weariness in the service of life? She didn't know, sought no further. She bent down again, found another tip of green and tenderly uncovered it to the light of day.

Some weeks later the weeds in Marta's garden also sprang to life. She should have known by now that once you become the ally of anything in this world you have a thousand enemies and no more peace. Marta, a friend to flowers, had discovered an enormous hostility toward them in the created universe.

On this May morning she directed her attack against the grass shoots within an enclosure of chicken wire where for nearly thirty years now she had been growing vegetables, yes, but flowers as well, scattered everywhere amidst these nourishing plants. Thus her dull life had had this richer side, a little mad and fanatical. In no time she had weeded out one row. By now she believed she could tell the difference between good and bad. Yet once, having allowed a certain weed to grow to maturity (at first mistaken for a domestic plant), she had watched how, under her care and watering, it flourished and grew beautiful and finally bore flowers shaped like tiny bells, as gracious and well made as those of her favourite plants. Perhaps, then, all beings in this world bore fruit according to the love spent on them.

That's how it went with her thoughts these days. She no longer had the strength for heavy tasks. Now she gave herself solely to her little garden, and as she did so her thoughts, like plants well cared for, also sprang free from silence and routine. They became company for Marta. It seemed to her that they were beautiful, each with its loneliness. Sometimes she was astonished to find they were her own. On that day a feeling crept into her heart that they were too lofty to have come from her alone. But from whom else could she have had them? Perhaps she had always had them, but locked deep inside her, as indistinct as the flower-to-come in the heart of a dull seed. And if she had not lost her robust health, if she had not felt the idea of her death flapping at her soul like a frightened moth, would she have paid the least attention to her thoughts, would she have known that hers was a human life?

Moving awkwardly on her knees, she cleared the earth around the cosmos. She spoke to the flowers the whole time, congratulating them on their good nature – flowers of the poor, making no demands, living in almost any soil, born again of seeds they had dropped in autumn. But no less than these she had loved certain of her plants that she had taken great pains to save. Something like an angry thought crossed her mind. Why, she wondered, should a small life as tranquil as a flower's have so many enemies?

Now look: there she was scratching at the earth around a peony, and a stalk detached from its root came away in her hand, cut through at its most sensitive point, just where it left the earth. Och, she thought in vexation, because of a greedy grub it's turned to worm now, and it could have been two or three great flowers, moist and proud. And what good did it do, for the worm itself will surely be eaten today! But it was she who found him in the dark earth and crushed him, almost with pleasure, beneath her heel. There was nothing left but to protect the other young plants and there was only one way, long and tiring, which she had been obliged to follow. Each year the flowers appeared to her as a wonder she would never see clearly enough; but the care they demanded was equally inexhaustible.

She went back inside the house to cut from cardboard what looked like little collars, and then out again to force them into the earth around the roots. This done, she stood up, her face somehow shrunken, sagging and a little empty from fatigue.

129

She still had to support the plants in their struggle against the wind, with sticks planted beside them and attached with a bit of string. She went about her task with deliberate slowness, carefully avoiding any sudden move that might revive the pain momentarily asleep in her right side. It was the pain that caused her to give the impression of bearing within her something fragile, of great value.

Far away Stepan passed, gave her an irritated glance, then went on his way, scattering to the ends of their land the raging sound of hostile words. The whole day long you could hear this indistinct grumbling sound that traced his path from one place to the next, now nearby, now almost indecipherable in the strong western wind, itself a great complainer.

Marta stood up for a moment to watch this man go past, her husband, her life's companion: was it really possible? And what kind of thing was young love that could sometimes join natures so completely opposite?

His intermittent growling was lost in the hot wind, which today for a change whispered of tenderness but as if that were a far country infinitely hard to reach.

She went inside and began the chore of preparing something for the man to eat. When the soup was ready she brought it to the table and neatly set the places. She wasn't going to give up good manners just because Stepan had turned into a savage. For a centrepiece she placed among the dishes some blue cornflowers in a little bowl that she had once painted with flowers, blue as well, for that was her favourite colour. Blue seemed to her to have a gentle, dreamlike quality, the colour of day – but of night as well under certain kinds of clouds or moonlight. She went to the doorway to call Stepan. He was nowhere to be seen, and as her gaze settled on the distance she forgot why she was there and realized that she was looking with a completely new thrill of attention at things that had surrounded her for years.

She would likely have been most surprised if a passer-by familiar with the ways of the Canadian West, wandering by some miracle this far along the dusty road, had been able to say at once that this was a Polish or Slavic farm. Differ though they might in some respects, all these farms had in common their small grove of aspen, the lower branches pruned to give free passage to the air and sun, and under them a hundred little coops, some for broody hens, others still for geese or young ducks held captive. In these thin copses, already sparse, there would often be horned animals that grazed and cleared the space still more. This was the kind of little wood that Marta saw to the east of the house, like a protection against the infinity of the plain. Alas, it had turned into a junk yard: carcasses of buggies without wheels forming little settees in which no one ever sat, and stranded sleds or cutters. Yet something light and singing went through the place, as if the wind, wherever in the world it might have been, whatever despair it might have known, grew tranquil and regained its calm on coming back to this little wood.

Not until today, after thirty years of living in Volhyn, did Marta realize that she and old Stepan, perhaps unwittingly, had reproduced almost exactly the atmosphere of the poor farm in their native Volhynia from which they had come. Almost the same farm this was but surrounded by a savage silence. How strange it seemed to her, all of a sudden! But what had captured her attention was today's very peculiar sound of air in motion. She listened, poised like someone listening to a voice, a distant call, and suddenly she was filled with living joy. In this warm noontime, barely tempered by a breeze just strong enough to make the aspens tremble, this was what she heard: the faint clicking of their leaves, like festive castanets. The same sound Marta remembered hearing in just such an aspen wood in Poland, when she was young and thinking only of the future. Oh, this dear aspen wood filled with music, she could count on it then to link her always with the wellspring of her life!

Then she remembered why she had come to the door and searched across the plain which seemed to be lying in a dream of expectation – she had never got over the notion, however often she looked out at it, that behind the emptiness someone was there. Not knowing where to direct her voice to reach Stepan, she simply shouted into the immensity: "Hey! Yaramko!"

That was what she called him these days. If she called him "Man!" as he nowadays said "Woman!" to her, it would have seemed an offence against their love of former years. On the other hand, a feeling of friendship still clung to the Christian name Stepan, and she could not bring herself to use it: it would have been like trying to call back a person who had long ceased to exist.

"Yaramko!" she shouted again. "Your soup!"

To make him come running there was really nothing left but this call to eat, as if he were a farm animal.

From the far fields, he straightened up and came toward her, a puny silhouette with short legs and large, bushy head. As a fly surrounds itself with buzzing, he walked surrounded by his own complaints, a constant, wearisome reiteration of wrongs, of defiance and threats directed at nothingness, grown to such a litany that he himself was perhaps no longer aware of it.

As he came alongside the little garden he stopped, saw where Marta had been working and seemed to take violent exception to it. He shook his head in a rage and broke out with a new attack of lamentations. Then, his cap pulled down to his ears, he sat down to eat, grabbed some bread and, as if this too was the object of his wrath, tore at it with his teeth.

Could this face that Marta saw before her still be called human? His forehead, his eyes, his mouth – features that even in the grimmest face would constitute a door of access – were concealed by hair. His great rake-like moustache covered the whole lower part of his face; the frightful briar patch of his hair spread daily on all sides, with enormous tangled eyebrows rising darkly to meet it; beneath them, deep-sunken wolf's eyes watched, black and defiant.

Tonight, thought Marta, she would dig out of her trunk their old wedding photograph so as to see Stepan's face and remind herself that this was indeed the man with whom, before the priest and for her lifetime, she had sworn an alliance of affection.

III

What kind of evenings did they spend together in Volhyn, in this season when evenings were long and astonishing pink skies hung in suspense over the darkened earth? From a pile of Ukrainian newspapers printed in Codessa Stepan would pull an old number – any one, he had read them all before. As he laboriously fitted words and phrases together he could still work himself into a rage at the absurd attempt of mankind everywhere to improve its lot.

Marta, for her part, would get out the Eaton's catalogue. For her it was a friend. It was from the catalogue that she had learned a few English words, though they were the farthest from the necessities of her life: dress, coat, hat, rug, curtains, garden swing. It was a good schoolmaster: it illustrated its words with pictures Marta could understand.

In the beginning, before it became a book of knowledge, it had perhaps, above all, been a book of covetousness. All she lacked at that time became clear to her as she leafed through this catalogue filled with pictures that made you want. This beautiful modern kitchen, for example, with a proper sink and gay plastic curtains; or that maroon coat with the fur collar. Marta had imagined that with such a coat she could run away from Volhyn, take her place in the civilized world and join her children who would no longer be ashamed of her. Now it was only the pages of garden seeds that made her heart beat with desire.

The catalogue opened of its own accord at these pages she had studied a hundred times. Once more she was touched at the infinite variety of flowers. She dreamed of seeing them this summer, perhaps her last, all represented in her garden.

Stepan rustled his paper, threw it aside, took the lamp and began to climb the stairs. She followed. The lamp blown out, they lay beside each other under the eiderdown of fine goose feathers sorted by hand. What had she not made with her hands? Pillows, also stuffed with goose down, coloured quilts, not to mention the thousands of meals she had prepared, and all the other thankless drudgery such as killing chickens or catching the warm blood of the still-screaming pig. If it had not been for her garden and her flowers, which testified in her favour, how much more terrified she might have been at the thought of leaving this world!

The night before her promised to be long, like a long journey of the soul turning, turning around itself. . . . The Eaton's book had taught her none of the words we call abstract. To recapture her thoughts of nostalgia and regret she had recourse to the old language of the Ukraine which she and Stepan would have used if they still used any with each other. Those feelings that we never express, that live crouched in the deepest crannies of the soul, that we never name – how do they manage not to die completely? Suddenly Marta was aware of the wind whining about the roof. She wondered if she was not already touched by the illness that would carry her off. Under her fingers, on her right side, was a tiny lump no bigger than a walnut. When she pressed it, the pain awoke.

And what would happen, she wondered, if she tried once more to make contact with Stepan, to confess her anxiety? What would happen then? Would he tell her to go and be looked after? But what for? She felt weary and discouraged at the thought of the long trip to Codessa, and then the train to McLennan where there was a little hospital. The worst cases were sent farther still, to Edmonton.

Edmonton, capital of Alberta, she rehearsed like a good schoolgirl who loses no opportunity of reinforcing a lesson learned.

Edmonton was, nonetheless, unreal to her. At times she had to make an effort to believe that beyond Volhyn there were cities and vast populations, and that all those things, the world and its countries and human societies, actually did exist.

Most of all she hated drawing attention to herself, having people fuss over her, perhaps being a nuisance. Her life didn't seem to be worth that trouble, and fear overcame her at the very notion of the slightest inconvenience she might cause. In fact, she could not follow too precisely what went on in her mind, and by dint of thinking silently to herself she came to be unsure of everything, even her melancholy.

Thus one night she reached the point of wanting to detach herself from all things so that nothing else would be taken from her. Her heart was like ice. No trace of a desire aroused her now. She even thought she might not plant flowers anymore. Good Lord, who would care? What passer-by, what other soul, would ever worry about the flowers at Volhyn!

But when summer came, under its excessive sun, there were perhaps more flowers than ever in this little garden at the end of the long dirt road from Codessa to Volhyn.

Lacking the strength to make rows or compose her intricate designs with groups of plants – diamonds, points or squares – that she had taken such pleasure improvising every spring, she had let them grow this time according to chance and providence, and the effect was perhaps the more striking because of it. Under giant clouds or a clear sky, the mass of packed and varied flowers mixing their brilliant colours formed a kind of serried round-dance, crying summer to the whole horizon.

Unable to go on caring for them, Marta now went near them only to rest and enjoy the show they made.

She would sit on a little stool right in their midst, closest to summer, in the very heart of this marvellous and incomprehensible summer. Yet she remembered how winter had piled the snow until the windows were covered; she remembered the fierce winds, she had not forgotten their fury. And she would sit there for hours, almost without moving, hands crossed on her knees, to all appearances just an old woman without much to expect of her life or of this world; but her soul, resolute and full of good will, was searching as it had never done before. She asked herself, gently astonished, "Summer, what is summer really?"

Pensively she considered this gilded light, this well-being of leaves and air, this health in all things, this fervent living, this joy, mute and secret, and said to herself, "Summer, summer, what is it anyway?"

Her white kerchief framed a face whose deep tan no longer disguised the clay-like tint that lay beneath, against which her eyes appeared each day to be a more striking blue. She looked again at her delicate poppies, her fragile snapdragons; she saw her flowers healthy and alive. A breeze stirred among them, and as they all together started tossing their heads they seemed to maintain that they were the true thing in this life:

its gentleness, its beauty, all its tenderness. Oh, the silly creatures! They seemed to claim they were the only ones who knew what it was about.

Marta caressed them with her hand as she would have caressed someone too innocent, too young to understand, such as a child. And were not flowers, in their innocence, a kind of eternal childhood of creation?

But when she caught herself thinking this way, in regions which she felt were so much beyond her, she would take herself to task: Stop that now. You'll never be any good at thinking. Stop it, it's not for you.

IV

A few days later she had the notion of bringing some of her scarlet lilies to the long-forgotten icons in the chapel. And away she went. Today the wind touched her lightly. Around her, as she walked with deliberate steps, one might have thought the wind indulged in mischievous games, now tugging upward at her long skirt, now raising little whorls of dust around her. Her lilies over her arm, her hair well hidden under the white kerchief, she made her way along this endless dirt road, straight and lonely as if it came from time's beginning. Marta contemplated the sky, so wide, and the horizon, so patient, and her own life, buried in so much silence that it seemed to have dissolved in it.

"What kind of life did you have anyway, Marta Yaramko?" she asked herself as candidly as if she had been talking to a mere acquaintance. But she didn't know what kind of life she'd had. The question is hard enough for anyone to answer. For her, with almost no points of comparison with other lives, the problem was insoluble.

But seeing herself underway on this long, long road which

after Codessa went on to other villages, bigger and bigger, and came at last to cities, she felt drawn onward, carried toward a human family, a murmur of voices. Notions of busy crowds awoke in her mind. She daydreamed of them as of something fantastic; she felt in her heart a little shock of adventure, of excitement. It seemed to her that she was travelling toward Canada.

She was a part of Canada, of course; somewhere, carefully tucked away, she even kept her naturalization certificate. To get it she had merely to declare before a witness that she loved the country and would be loyal to it. But Canada seemed to her less a country than an immense map with strange cut-outs, especially in the North; or was it no more than a sky, a deep and dream-filled waiting, a future in suspense? Sometimes it seemed her life had been spent on the edge of the country, in some vague zone of wind and loneliness that Canada might yet embrace. For how could those in Volhyn, now reduced to a handful, old and complaining, have reached out and touched it? They were no longer quite Ukrainian but not quite Canadian either, poor lost folk, so discouraged it seemed there was no way they could help themselves except perhaps by disappearing.

She raised a baffled gaze to the sky, wide and immense.

"It's your fault as well," she reproached it, "you let us stray. You held back. It's true, it is!" she tried to explain, as if to someone or something. "We came into the world in our little villages in Poland, living on top of each other, where you could hear the neighbours crying or laughing in their house. And next thing you know we're lost away here in so much silence and sky, our lives small and forgotten as those of insects.

"You ask all the questions," she protested to the sky, "but do you ever give an answer? Will you ever tell us why we came so far, what wind blew us here, what we're doing here, the poor of the Ukraine, in these farthest prairies of Canada?"

Then, tired and upset at having dared to think such high-flown thoughts, she brought her attention back to her surroundings. On both sides of the road the grasses waved in the wind. Used to rougher treatment, today they bent gently over, and their furry heads in ripe, half-moulting panicles formed a golden florescence as far as you could see, a blond froth floating on the surface of their endless movement.

And Marta's heart melted in a mysterious way, as if in this eternal play of wind and grass and sunlight there was for her an inexhaustible consolation.

V

The state of disrepair in the little chapel shocked her deeply – though she should have expected it, for she was the only one in recent times to have cleaned it up at all. Dust, ruins, silence! You could no longer make out the faces of the saints in the pictures they had brought along from Volhynia to have these uncertain friends at their sides in the great uprooting. Who had withdrawn? God, forgetting his creatures lost in the depths of the Canadian waste? Or they themselves, the humans, through a failure of the imagination? Who could understand these things, she wondered; but at once renounced the dizzying thought. Then memories awoke in her heart, just as, encouraged by the silence on the edge of humid marshlands, innumerable birds arise out of the grasses, out of their sleep.

Her youth appeared to her: confident, daring to the point of foolhardiness. She was the one who had wanted to leave and prodded at Stepan's will, for he was frightened by the long journey toward the unknown. She was the one who had swept him along in the ardour of her faith in this still undiscovered country, about which they had known nothing but its name and immensity.

She remembered the amazement that had overcome them as day after day they rolled in their immigrants' train across an unchanging landscape.

She tried to remember how all those things had come about – the journey, their arrival, the frenzied pace of their labours. But that whole human adventure was so impregnated with silence that even those who had lived through it wondered about its reality. It was as if they had entered alive into a kind of limbo, between this life and the Eternal. How could you deal with such solitude? Yet they had tried. Oh yes! No one could reproach them for not trying, with their bare hands if need be, to create in this silence of God and man their little tender life, intimate and domesticated. But what were a dozen houses here, and their few children – whom the country had in any case quickly claimed as its own?

How could Marta, at twenty, have been expected to understand her heart's longing for those enormous distances, those wide horizons – she who now knew their frightful boredom! She looked again at the icons. In their first days at Volhyn, when they were young and enterprising and thought they could tame the prairie, they had built this little chapel far from their cabins, leaving room around it for the village they liked to think would take life and shape in these vast, empty fields. When they had their chapel, a priest would surely come: that was their simple reckoning, their naïve conviction. But no priest ever came, except the one from Codessa to bless the grave of someone out here; and as soon as the rites were accomplished he fled from the place, for it inclined men to see themselves as transients of a single day, here in this world.

Then Marta grew attentive to a breath of air trembling on the threshold; it was the wind, seemingly astonished to find this long-locked door standing open. You'd think it was shy about coming in, though filled with curiosity. "What's going on today?" the wind seemed to whisper.

And Marta smiled as if a friendly soul had made a little sign to her. Nothing could be more caressing and enchanting than the wind, so often furious in this country. All the moods of the spirit, the sterile revolt of man that disturbs the mind almost to madness; the great waves of boredom that wash in from all sides; but also the relaxation, the gentleness and calm – it seemed as if the wind contained all these and tried to express them, one after the other. It must know our souls or something of what goes on there, Marta thought to herself at times. How else could it be so changeable, so impetuous, sometimes submissive, but always searching, searching. "What are we searching for, will you tell me?" she asked, as if she and the wind were trying to solve the same riddle. Then in a lively voice she invited it: "Well, come in, won't you?"

And as if the sound of that human voice had really called the wind, it crossed the threshold. Light and singing, sweet smelling from its journey across the plains, timid and joyful at once, a breeze invaded the narrow chapel. She heard it leap from one side to the other, bounce gently off the walls, lift a scrap of paper from the floor, then freeze in some corner like a playing child who pretends he is unseen.

"You're feeling young today," she told the wind. "You've forgotten the troubles of the world."

It was amazing how much in creation made her think of childhood: flowers, the wind sometimes and birds. For her, what was old was winter, anger, boredom. Summer and tenderness were unalterably young.

Suddenly her three little ones were before her eyes – had she ever really had them to herself except when they were very small? Just long enough to teach them the speech of the

Ukraine, a few songs, a few dances from Volhynia, and the government had taken them away, teaching them English, shaping them in its own way for a life quite different from the one she could have offered. What should she have done? Follow the path of the younger generation? Go to school herself? Perhaps, but it would have been too hard; she and Stepan were already too stupefied by drudgery, too worn out for that new, desperate effort. And now they were irrevocably separated, she in Volhyn and her children somewhere far away, leading the life of the times. Could she blame them? Marta tried to imagine how it might have been if she'd appeared at home in her own mother's lifetime, seeing that old woman, so stubborn, so ignorant that she'd predicted to the young couple about to leave for Canada: "You'll never get there. There's a great abyss somewhere, you'll fall into it."

Marta trembled. She realized that her children, if they were now with her and old Stepan, would feel as estranged as she herself would under the thatched roof where she was born. She caught herself weeping softly. She saw herself, as it were, without parents and without children. What was the reason for such loneliness? Too much progress, and too fast? Or not enough? All she could seem to glimpse was that one day descendants of hers far enough from their origins to feel sure of themselves in this country would perhaps not be ashamed of their old immigrant grandmother. She smiled in her heart at these strangers, one of whom she could hear asking, "Our little old grandmother Yaramko, what was she really like?"

At last she left off crying and said, as if excusing herself for a fault, "It's the sickness does that." And as she looked again at the icons she was suddenly resentful of them. They were Ukrainian saints. What did they know about the life of immigrants in Canada? Or about life, for that matter!

But she was afraid that with such ideas she might irritate

145

them more. What was the good of thinking anyway? That wasn't why she had come here. She just wanted to tidy the place a little, that was all she seemed good for anymore.

She arose, fetched a pail from behind the altar and crossed a corner of prairie to fill it at the creek. The whole meadowland was covered with high grasses of many kinds, unified and mixed together by their rustling sound and their tireless waving to and fro. When her pail was filled she went back along the path she had trodden on the way. In the high heavens the wind was passing, leaving among the clouds the same quiet waves as down below among the grasses. The breathing of this immense and – today at least – placid solitude soothed her mind and its torment of identity. The whole world was lonely, after all, and blessed in spite of it. Besides, it was such a relief not to hear old Stepan grumbling. It was he who had cursed and rejected their children for following their own destinies. Ah, that's no way to act, she reproached him in her thoughts (the only way she ever reached him now: what was the use?).

She looked around her at the waving grass. The slim ears of wood millet, the hairy fescue grass, this great sea of wild grain swept in an unending swell. And this, which she had seen a thousand times, caught her attention again and lightened her heart. Once again the thought crossed her mind that the plain was deep in a great dream of things to come, and was singing of patience, with the promise that all things, in their time and place, would yet be accomplished.

Kneeling on the floor, she attempted to make it shine as it once had. What for? Not for the Lord, at any rate. Supposing he was alive and present, she imagined he would feel more at home outside, on the wind's wings in the cool air, than in this little chapel where the smell of must would outlast all her efforts. Not for the future either did she scrub this floor.

Without its children, Volhyn had no more than a few years, months perhaps, to live. Maybe Volhyn would die for all time on the day she herself disappeared. Perhaps in the last analysis she was washing here only to ensure Volhyn an end that was clean and worthy. So that no one could say, "Volhyn died before Marta."

Her task at an end, she cast a final glance at the icons, whose eyes, dusted clean, could now see how little help they had brought.

She withdrew a step or two, gave them a nod, not quite a friendly one, just polite, then closed the door behind her as she left. And the wind, which had scurried after her along the ground, followed her off, as if today it went everywhere with Marta.

VI

But the Volhyn wind does not long remain the friend of grasses or flowers or the soul that loves and nurtures life. From the side of the distant Rockies it came down in searing gusts one day. Under a darkened sky it stirred and whirled the flying earth reduced to finest dust.

Marta, grieved by the mistreatment her flowers would suffer, tried to come to their rescue. With bits of string she forced the gladioli to submit to their supporting sticks. She herself could barely withstand the attack of the wind and the lumps of earth it tossed in her face; how would the flowers fare on their tender stalks? Her pain, rebelling against the effort she was making, rose against her, rapping at her side with tiny, hard, well-placed blows. "Will you stop!" she said, vexed. "Have I time for you just now?"

No more than two steps from her house, battling against the wind, she resembled some blurred human form caught in a desert dust storm; and the flowers around her, all bent in the same direction, were like lopsided butterflies.

When she had safely anchored her gladioli it seemed unfair

not to do the dahlias. Having gone to the rescue of a few of her creatures, how could she ignore the others? They might notice! Not until she had given the whole garden what protection she could did Marta herself take shelter. Standing at her little window which was almost obscured by the storm, her face against the pane, she watched her flowers' tormented dance in the gloomy, thickened air until at last they too turned grey under their coat of dust, like the sky and air around them. Occasionally one, torn loose, would rise in a whirl as if in an invisible spiral.

Then, waiting for the storm to end, Marta sat down, crossed her hands and remembered how this little garden was born and grew, for in a sense it told the real history of her life.

At that time they had not been long in Volhyn. Everything was still to be done. They had nothing but a shelter, camping in a shanty that barely kept out the rain, with a few chickens, a cow and their babies. They were short of everything, and Stepan that day was about to set off on the stiff forty-mile trip to buy the things they needed most urgently. On the point of leaving he had asked, "Do you want anything else now, besides the sugar and salt and bread?" In those days he was a fairly good husband, asking about her wants in a tone that was still well-meaning.

It was spring, an immense springtime of mud, of almost liquid earth, with a lofty sky that was reflected in a thousand unsewed patches. "What else do you need?" With this memory a smile came to Marta's face, a smile of compassion and friendship for what she had been in those hard times. Wouldn't it have been simpler to ask what she could do without? The list of indispensable things had grown so long! Discouraged at having to choose, she had looked around at the mud and the endless unfurling of the desolate naked plain that surrounded and laid siege to their shanty. As soon as you stepped outside you sank into sticky clay that clung to your soles in heavy clumps. That was when she had the idea of bringing her first garden flowers to this lonely land: sunflowers, maybe poppies too.

Surprisingly, Stepan had no objection, and brought back what garden seeds he could, seven or eight little envelopes that produced a fine harvest and plenty of new seeds to plant. The following summer these formed a harmony of colours that immediately seemed at home, as much so as the horizon or the clouds. A house in its own place, a flower where it belongs, a tree where one is needed – what was the meaning of all that? Marta had often wondered, without ever finding an answer that satisfied her.

But do wonders not bring other wonders? One evening, a few years later, a stranger – they never found out anything about him or what chance brought him so far into that country – a stranger came along the bumpy road in a little car that sat high on its wheels. At the sight of her giant sunflowers and shining poppies he stopped and got out of the car. He approached the flowers and greeted them with an astonishment that his hasty movements betrayed. He bent down, plucked a gillyflower, examined it closely and smiled. Finally he turned toward the wretched hut a gaze that called for an answer.

Marta, who was spying through the little window, felt that she had to go out. At once the stranger began speaking volubly to her. She did not understand his language. In her turn she spoke in Ukrainian, but he too failed to understand. They looked at each other in embarrassment. But Marta would have sworn that this man felt indebted to her for a sudden buoyancy of spirit. Was it the flowers? But how could he take them as a personal offering? Could it be that for certain souls confidence in life, wherever found, came as a precious gift? If so, they themselves must be generous and noble, Marta had said to herself.

Well, about six months later they received – from the stranger, beyond a doubt, but with no letter or explanation – a little package of bulbs that had sat for a long time in the Codessa post office.

Marta looked up, searching in the whirling dust outside for the countless purple dahlias that had come from those dozen bulbs, and the gladioli too, whose shining white still showed in glimpses through the opaque light.

"And what about the story of the rose I had from Lubka!" she said.

From that dear old friend in Codessa, whom she had not been able to visit, alas, for so long, she had received a rose of India taken from her garden. It was pressed between two blank pages as a kind of letter – for Lubka, poor soul, had never learned to write. From this one flower, hung from her ceiling to dry – head down, as it should be – Marta had been able to recover some three hundred seeds, which had given Volhyn almost as many roses, and each of these in turn had produced its hundreds.

Marta lost herself in her calculation of the infinite descendants of a single flower. She entered into the contemplation of such munificence as into a dream, beautiful and absurd. One hand on her ailing side, her eyes fixed in a deep reverie, she listened, no longer discouraged, to the howling, hot wind from the west. Neither wind nor tempest nor any winter could ever prevail against the gentle will to live of these lovely things she saw on earth!

Now drought descended on the tortured country. With so many grievous sights in the world, how can we find in

151

ourselves room for regrets or compassion for mere flowers? Sitting in the oppressive heat on the bench beside the house, almost as crushed as the few flowers that had survived the storm, time and again Marta was on the point of fetching some water for them. But the only water was in the dug-out, a kind of pond hollowed to hold the rainfall for the animals during torrid summers. It was far away, on the only sandy spot of their farm, about a quarter of a mile off. There were moments when Marta dreamt sweetly that the thing was done: she had dragged herself thither, brought back two pailfuls and distributed the water as fairly as she could. But then her eyes opened on the drooping leaves and corollas and she felt almost bitter against these creatures, always calling on her for this or that. Weren't they all going to die in any case, with the autumn's first frost? What was so important about keeping them alive an extra day?

But finally off she went. Which will go first, she wondered, me or the garden? And in spite of everything, her heart hoped it would be the garden, so that when she herself went she would have no worries over it.

Far away in the fields Stepan looked up. He saw this spectacle: the old woman – and there was no doubt she had suddenly grown very old – with her two pails, struggling with all her body as if to pass through an invisible wall. What madness was this? When everything was perishing with heat, thirst and despair, and life was an immense, dust-ridden exile, how could anybody still worry about a few wretched flowers? Now it was flowers, in the old days it had been songs and music. He was slowly grasping, and had been for some time, the way in which Marta had always been his enemy, loving life as she did despite the bitter blows it had rained upon them. He was seized by a kind of jealousy and fury, seeing only evil intentions around him. He would show this old woman what he could do when pushed to it. Either she would declare herself for him and against life, or he would have his vengeance. Indeed, on days like this, with the wind always from the same quarter and always whining, plaintive and exasperated, on days like this, filled from morning to night with a raging discontent, Stepan Yaramko went almost mad. And he looked like a madman, the way he suddenly grasped his tousled head to squeeze out of it the boredom and the wind's howling and his sickly thoughts. A few minutes later he ran to hitch Ivan, the black horse, to the buggy. Formerly high-spirited, Ivan was now almost as brutish as his master.

Marta saw the rig go by adding its own cloud of dust. Stepan, standing up, was lashing with the reins. With raucous cries, like a cossack on his mount, he sent Ivan at a gallop on the road to Codessa.

He's dying of drought as well, she thought, and he's going to what his demon tells him is salvation and well-being. But alcohol will never do more than consume still further his poor, half-burnt-out soul.

VII

When he was well on his way, Stepan, who had shouted his
lungs out at his horse, at himself and at the wind, finally sat
down and collapsed into a shapeless mass, his eyes reddened,
his eyelids and whole face coated with dust. He seemed
dazed. After his rages he often fell into a state of gloom and
stupor. At such times he might remain for hours only half
conscious of what he did or said or even thought – for he
followed his thoughts from afar, disinterested, as if they
barely belonged to him. Even the certainty of having lived
escaped him, or his life appeared to him at best like a long,
monotonous day, a day some thirty years long and without
milestones, without events, except perhaps for the distant
scene which he now recaptured with some clarity: famine was
raging in Volhynia; his kin had begun to show the hideous
symptoms of chronic hunger, their features hollowed, their
ribs protruding, their bellies swollen, and an expression in
their eyes which had never left him, despite the dull unifor-
mity of so many unchanging days.

Then a great blur of space and time panned before him. He was suddenly in the midst of fields of tall, ripe wheat. A threshing machine was rumbling. The grain trickled out in an inexhaustible stream; it filled carts and granaries and more granaries until it had to be left running out on the ground, exposed to the coming winter. No one knew what to do with it. The same frightful abundance was everywhere. The incredible harvest of that year was baffling; they had talked of burning the surplus. And about that time a letter arrived from Volhynia. It told him of his mother's death, which came as an end result of the famine. To keep his wheat from moulding and complete loss, Stepan fed it to his pigs. Thus two things were strangely connected in his memory: the letter from Volhynia along with the distraught look of hungry faces; and then the brimming trough and the avid guzzling of the swine, their little eyes shining with pleasure.

What more did he remember of the long, dry, windy day that was his life? A harsh, brilliant sunlight; then sudden, furious storms, brutal cold and so much snow that everyone in Volhyn was prisoner in his house for weeks at a time, with no news even of his nearest neighbour. Again the contrasts, again their unreality: it was enough to make a man doubt his own common sense, his very existence. And it was at the end of a life like that, as if to give thanks, that Marta was still watering her flowers.

Stepan trembled and came back to the present under the shock of his resentment. He whipped his horse a few times, shifted in his seat and suddenly wailed aloud. He grudged the joy of others in a life that he himself would have liked to see accursed.

You passed a few houses, then for a long time you rode through a marshy zone, low-lying land and damp, with rotting reeds and a smell of slime, where the frightened cries of birds went crossing at intervals. Stepan sank deeper into his mood, lost in a somnolence of the mind where scarcely anything could reach him.

But suddenly a child's face moved in the mist of his reflections, appearing as much alive as if it had emerged that moment from the grasses of the marsh. Little bare feet were dancing on the beaten earth in front of a poor shanty; the little girl's braids, too, danced around her head. Stepan almost called out "Irina!" Stalked by tenderness, he put a hand to his moustache, which he twirled, then he drove the memory off with a flood of rancorous reproaches. Children! They were no children of his, he wanted no part of them – the girl with her conceited airs and the others stuck up as young lords. They had shown up at Volhyn only to give advice: "You should do it this way, that's not the way to farm, this is how you go about it. . . ." Or there'd be messages scribbled in English on a postcard, with "Best regards, happy memories," and even from time to time a real letter addressed only to Mrs. Yaramko. Stepan had intercepted the last one, thrown it in the fire. That would teach them to take sides against him with Mrs. Yaramko.

But what if she were really sick, sick enough to leave this world! How could be find out? Life is a mystery and illness a greater one. Everything is mystery. A touch of anxiety crossed Stepan's mind in rapid flight. It was not quite grief, nor yet regret, but closer to fear, a vague feeling which he could not grasp.

At last he was out of the hateful marshland, with the hissing of its whip-like grass and its fetid odour. The air grew cleaner, the landscape changed. Stepan was entering a fertile region. Farmhouses appeared, well-kept ones, surrounded by havens of green that kept them sheltered from the wind, houses and barns properly placed, with metal-winged windmills to pump water from the ground or even generate electricity.

Bitter resentment seized Stepan. He saw fences that outlined the groups of farm buildings with perfect neatness. In front of some houses, more like city than farm dwellings, a tractor would stand or a big red truck, sometimes even a new car, its body glinting in the sun.

That won't last, he was going to say, as he often did to console himself. But he quickly saw that this prosperity was there to stay, this fine easy life Ukrainians led nowadays; and they owed it largely to the frantic efforts of the pioneer era, this generation reaping in joy what had been sowed in bitterness by the one before. Rolling his eyes in stupefaction, Stepan felt himself a victim of the greatest possible injustice.

Sounds of voices and human activity pierced through his musings. He was coming into Codessa. As he looked up he was disconcerted. . .as if he were arriving in a village for the first time in his life and had never seen anything like it. Not that the village was very lively on such a hot, windy afternoon. The infinite silence and wildness of the plain still crept too close for that. But its pathetic reminder only emphasized the sight – between two glimpses of the infinite – of a wide commercial street that, in two blocks, concentrated almost all the business section of Codessa. The sign of a little printer's shop, a shoemaker's, a movie house, two banks side by side, the window of one of those self-service stores where you saw the stock laid out in long rows. Then the town offices set up in a kind of barn, and those of the Department of Agriculture right beside it, not much better housed. Farther on, the cleaners and dyers, a garage with gas pumps, an auto junk yard and finally, back there a little, the elongated dome of the curling rink. This was the heart of Codessa. Stepan blinked, astounded. He couldn't get over it.

Yet, no doubt because of the violent heat, most people were holed up in their houses. With its banks, its store, its garage almost empty for the moment, Codessa seemed to have risen from the earth for one brief instant to a life with no reality.

Stepan climbed down in front of the beer parlour, tied his horse to a hitching post and disappeared into the dark interior

A few old faces invaded by whiskers, their gaze perpetually lost, looked lazily up at him, in questioning rather than in greeting.

"Good day, Yaramko of Volhyn," he heard from this one from that one.

He mumbled some vague, churlish reply, sat down and began to drink.

A little later, with the help of alcohol, words came back to him. And there it was he'd let it slip out: Marta was sick. A first he might have thought it was a trick for getting out of hard work and doing what she pleased. That's what he had thought. Now he wasn't so sure. Maybe she was really sick. She'd changed her ways. Almost good-natured these days. And everybody knew how she used to be, eh? Jealous and hot tempered as they come.

Then he fell silent again and began to see the possible truth in what he had just said. He should have held his tongue. As long as a thing was left unsaid you could pretend you didn't know it, pretend it wasn't there.

His suspicious eyes spied at the faces around him, strayed to the rectangle of light at the doorway. He made signs to himself as if swearing to hold his tongue. Who could a person talk to, anyway? Was there a listener on earth that you could trust? Despite himself he risked his luck with words again. His tongue was thick now, his eyes vague.

"Maybe," he said, "maybe Marta's going to die."

And he sat stunned as he realized that he'd known this all along.

"She just wants first chance at laying complaints," he said. "I know her. She always wanted to be the first to go. Get a head start on me. So she could blab all the things she has against me. That's how Marta is."

He stared at one drinker, then another. They'd begun to show some interest. His stare was watchful, sly and imploring at the same time.

"Hey you, Fedor," he said, addressing one of the old men who had come from Volhynia at the same time as himself. "Do you believe old women who die before us find anybody there to listen to them whine? Is anybody there at all?"

And Stepan began laughing aloud, wiping off his moustache wet with beer. He thought, Marta's leaving her precious garden now and going to milk the cows. That'll teach her. That'll teach her.

"Well, Fedor?"

In silence Fedor seemed to be searching the bottom of his glass for an answer to this embarrassing question. He was a frail old man of the first group to arrive, those who were forced almost without tools to invent a shelter and a few daily tasks, something measurable, vulnerable and human within the wide spaces, the unchanging horizons. He had been left with a feeling of bewilderment, an idea of the futility of human undertakings. Now he drank his old-age pension in three days and lived the rest of the time off a bitter little wine he made from wild berries. He slept beneath a tin roof at the edge of the village, in a kind of shack put together from odds and ends. It kept him more or less sheltered from the winds. Within hearing distance of the eternal silence, he had retained a taste for dangerous speculation. What should these poor people seek if not what lay at the bottom of that silence?

"Does anybody listen to the women there?" Fedor repeated at last. "Do you mean God? Could be, yes, it could be, Stepan Yaramko."

Everyone was listening carefully now to hear what the old man would say.

"God has to listen to somebody," Fedor began tentatively. "That's all right. He doesn't listen to the living. Not that I know of, anyway. When we're dead he has to listen. That's what I think. You see," he went on, noting that the others were looking on approvingly, "the Lord needs to know more about us men. And where could he find out if not from the dead souls when they come before him?"

"Tattlers, are they?" someone asked.

"Witnesses, I'd call them," said Fedor. "To my notion, that's where our Lord gets his information. It's true information he gets that way. Perhaps the only truth. For where," he demanded, growing more animated, "is the Judge going to get the exact truth? Not from the living! They all lie more or less, we know that. Where did you ever see," he asked, turning to Stepan, "a live man that wasn't some kind of a liar? As long as we live, we lie."

Stepan hunched down in his chair. Ah, it was true: one lived and lied. But did we lie for pleasure or because we were uncertain about things? And now Marta was going to testify against him. Patient, quiet, busy with her flowers? Oho! She was acting exactly like someone who's sure of having the Judge's ear before too long.

Suddenly he struck the table violently. He couldn't let that happen! Was there no way to shut her mouth? He'd managed to shut her up around the house for years now.

Ah yes, it may be possible on earth, said Fedor. Afterward it's not so easy.

Almost completely drunk by now, Stepan was making a

160

remendous effort to follow the flight of a maddened fly by listening to its buzzing. Suddenly the vague outline of an idea empted him, like a revenge. What if he had her looked after, his poor old woman? What if he took her to Edmonton, to the surgeons if need be? It would take every cent he had, and he saw himself reduced to beggary, his savings sacrificed in vain, for Marta would surely never get well enough to help again with the heavy chores. Did an old woman grow young after the hospital? Did a wasted woman grow robust and alert once more? Tears came to his eyes. Held back at the edge of his lashes, they revealed better than his gaze where his eyes were hidden, deep in the grass-like growth of his face. He sniffled once more, his head nodded. Soon he was half asleep, his elbows on the table, his forehead hidden in his hands.

VIII

Twilight had come long ago. A grave and touching illumi
nation spread over the western slope of the sky. The very
horizon seemed unable to tear itself away from the contem
plation of its own enchantment. At this hour – Marta'
favourite – she remained sitting with her face to the red sky
wondering over the meaning of this incandescence agains
which everything on earth shows black and seems more than
ever transitory, more than ever magnificent. The prairie a
this time of day appeared to grow wider, if that were possible
yet the human soul was perhaps more confident for all that.

But little by little Marta became conscious of the long
complaint of the animals penned in the corral. Stepan ha
gone off without thinking of them, and the cows were suffer
ing from their swollen udders. Poor things! Wasn't it enough
that they had to live just to serve the needs of men? Did we
have to let them suffer too, and them without the power o
reason?

She went off to get her pails and crossed the grassy prairi
to where the animals stood lowing in their pen, their head

turned toward the house. At night when the window was lit by the flame of the lamp, you would have said their call had a different tone, perhaps that of confidence.

In other times milking had been one of the more agreeable chores for Marta. She would sit on a low stool, her forehead against the animal's warm flank and feel beneath it the rumblings of inner rumination. The milk spurting at the side of the pail at first made a clear, high-pitched sound that afterwards grew thicker. True, she'd be pestered by flies and insects of all kinds and often cruelly stung; but the work gave you time to gaze around at the countryside, and it was then that Marta had most intensely felt its beauty. She remembered curious and unexpected surges of happiness, like gusts of perfume carried across the fields, all the more memorable because they were unexpected. For a long time during her life of ceaseless labour those moments had been her only ones of relaxation. She still remembered a cow that had been particularly gentle and obedient. She had only to tell her, "Stop that, keep your tail still!" and the little red cow would protest only with her ears, constantly waggling, even in the worst of fly-time.

When she was ready to carry back the brimming pails, Marta stopped, finding it absurd to use her last reserve of strength to retain a drop of milk or anything that she could not take with her forever. Her life had been made of the need to do just that. Yet she would not be able to take her flowers long. What then had made her sacrifice herself for them? she wondered, but found no good answer. No doubt it would take another to answer all the questions she had to ask.

She let the cows drink the milk she had just taken from them, keeping a little at the bottom of the pail for the cat and also for the "old bear." Sick from his binge, he might be glad to find a small jar of milk set to cool.

She bent down to get through the barbed wire. After the stubbly grass of the corral, the prairie was soft underfoot. At one time they'd planted timothy hay, but the ancient grasses had regained the upper hand: the meadow cat's tail, the purplish bent grass, twitch grass, lyme grass with its stiff ears, and foxtail – a great herbaceous mass pervaded by a constant breath of life. Even on a calm evening like this the whole plain was gently waving and a long, slow swell left for the far-off horizon. At this late hour of summer, of her life, Marta marvelled again at the face so delicate yet impenetrable that Volhyn's solitude had taken on for her.

Back at the house, she dropped heavily to the bench by the wall, suddenly feeling all the fatigue of the effort she had made. Her exhaustion was so great she feared she would never get her thoughts together again. She could barely perceive them; they were still too far, and they took on the form of dreams rather than reflections: vague, friendly shadows seeming to deal one way or another with their deep astonishment at this strange human life.

She went inside and drank a mouthful of cooled-off tea. Then, a little bowl of curds in her hand, she came out to the threshold to eat a few spoonfuls and look pensively at the lovely side of the sky, still pink, while the rest was already dipped in the deepest black. Under her white kerchief not much could be seen of her face except her eyes fixed with strange insistence on that lively tint in the sky, a last pulsing of red and gold melted together like a sleep embellished with dreams.

Marta went in again, rinsed out her bowl and tidied the small kitchen. It was a pleasant room, a little anxious, for it seemed to remember that a soul at grips with loneliness had tried humbly to beautify everything around her in her wish

164

to escape. In other years Marta had painted it delphinium blue, with a narrow border in pale yellow halfway up the wall. From the low ceiling with its heavy beams hung braids of onions, bundles of drying poppyheads and ears of corn tied in sheaves, giving off a light smell of autumn. The old peasant cupboards, formerly painted blue like the walls, were decorated with designs she had done from a pattern. The table was covered with an oilcloth with big red flowers on a blue-and-yellow background. All these colours were slowly dying but sometimes, such as now, the lamplight ephemerally brought them back to life in a last, feeble effort at revival.

Marta returned to the doorway. It occurred to her to look far out across the plain to a lonely tree that she had always known. The night was now dark blue. Against this background everything turned to a silhouette, and she easily spied the little tree, far as it was. With its foliage pulled over it like a cape and its lower branches like striding legs, it had always seemed to her to be walking, perhaps a monk, perhaps a pilgrim, but someone who had trudged a great distance. Time and again Marta had come to the doorway just to descry in the distance that walking silhouette, always bowed under its tireless efforts. Had anyone else ever had such a strange companion? In her mind she had turned it into everything imaginable: a peddler with a few rare flower seeds in his pack, or perhaps someone who had seen her children and was bringing news of them.

Then she turned to see the frail aspen grove. Tonight it was making a gentle noise, like the voices of a group of people speaking softly, cordially, in the dark.

With no instrument but these trees, the air had invented so many sounds that gladdened your heart! Marta tried to remember all of them but it was impossible. Often the trees had imitated rain so skilfully you were completely fooled; and then they'd make their leaves rattle like the castanets of some distant, youthful feast; sometimes their soft rustling had made her think of sympathy for human suffering.

Nor did Marta forget to greet the giant sky which dipped so low tonight and lit its stars so close you could have taken them for window lights on the endless Volhyn plain. Was this an image of the future that Marta saw? Could the world's loneliness at last be filled?

She pushed the heavy door shut with her knee to make sure it was home in its ill-fitting frame. She started up the steep stairway with its sharp turn at the landing. There she caught her breath for a moment and thought about great, strange things; for above this narrow staircase she saw as never before the immensity of the sky. She climbed the remaining steps. She changed the linen, lay down on the bed and, her eyes on the ceiling, experienced again the feel of the vast, living sky she had just seen.

"Why, oh why, did I have my life?" asked Marta.

IX

Coming in the house on some pretext or other around eleven that morning, Stepan cocked his head, listened, but heard no sound from the room beneath the roof. What could she be doing? Wasn't she going to come down and look after him as well as herself? What was the meaning of this immobility? Was she going to stay in bed for good?

He went out again and pretended to busy himself with one of the innumerable chores awaiting him, though they had all been neglected so long that perhaps it wasn't worth starting. Could he even save a bit of his harvest, dried out where it stood? Things had gone to the dogs here for too long. What could one man do alone with no help against such a load of work? Might as well let the work pile up and bury you right away, up to your neck, and never lift a finger. But what about Marta? Was she hungry? Would it be fitting for him to bring her something? A man serving a woman! The world upside-down, eh?

He came back toward the house, went inside and over to the foot of the stairs to listen for any sign of life upstairs, holding his breath. Still nothing. Should he go and look? That was an unpleasant thought. Once upstairs, what would he say? He'd have to mumble something or other, ask a question at least. He thought it over, his mouth under the thick moustache forming grimaces of objection. Fedor had maintained there was only one way to buy the silence of those about to leave this world: that was to speak as freely to them as if speaking were no concession. But Fedor was a widower and could say what he pleased. Who could be sure?

Finally Stepan put water to boil, threw in a handful of oatmeal. When the brew began to thicken he poured it into a bowl, stuck a spoon in it, added a little milk and started upstairs, clearing his throat to announce his coming. He hoped things would go well, that he wouldn't have to say a word. For what could he say? What name would he use? Just "Marta"? Impossible! He'd lost that habit too long ago. It would be as embarrassing as if he turned up shaved in front of her.

He arrived at the top of the stairs, looked sideways at Marta in her bed, put the bowl of oatmeal in her hands. He had thought of saying, Eat a little something, but even that was beyond his power. She looked up at him perplexed and seemed to be on the point of speaking. But speech was difficult for her too. She took the spoon, tasted the gruel, took another spoonful.

Well, it was eatable, maybe it tasted good, and she'd likely finish it off as soon as his back was turned. Then she'd get her strength again. Perhaps he could even save her now that he'd set his hand to it. So there wasn't such a hurry about committing himself with words.

He went downstairs and was about to head out to the fields again, perhaps to harness himself to this chore or that – one would do as well as the next and none would get him very far. Then he saw the chickens having a fine time in the garden! Scratch here, scratch there, get that root up, no, that one! Tear off that stem. . . . A hundred times a day until now he had seen Marta running, waving her apron to chase the intruders with cries that rose almost to a wail. Suddenly, without realizing it, he began to do the same, charging the fowl head down, waving his arms. When he had them back in their pen he saw that it was full of holes. He straightened a picket, tried to bend it to cover another breach left by another crooked picket. The whole place here, the fields, the buildings, matched the state of this wretched coop. Was it worth patching? As he tried to block a gaping escape hole he raised his head, suddenly suspicious again, and saw Marta's white face at the window. So she still placed some hope in him. He abandoned the chicken pen and went off with rapid strides, under the sky lowering with a coming storm, grumbling aloud in great waves of discontent. Where could he start? What was best? Could he still mow a patch of wheat? Why not? But a broken part from the mower had not come back from the repair shop, and he'd forgotten to ask in Codessa if he could still count on it. For that matter, thinking of his feuds with everyone in Volhyn, would he find anyone to come and thresh it for him?

A little later Marta heard again beneath her window the familiar grumbling voice accompanied by a great sound of straining and bumping. She pulled the curtain back and saw Stepan clearing up the little grove – their grove, just as in Poland. Surprise made her face turn paler than before. Grunting to encourage himself, Stepan was hauling out and piling up for a bonfire all the broken boxes, the buggy seat with its torn leather, the rubber boots in shreds, and heaven knew what else – broken cans, rusted gratings, in short, the whole junk heap! And the grove was beginning to breathe. It reappeared slowly as it had been in the first years of its life, pure, young and open, so that you could see through beneath its branches to the luminous prairie in the distance. And Marta drew a deep and easy breath, as if, with the aspen grove cleared, she finally saw accomplished one of the last commands of her own fate.

X

The summer in Volhyn seemed to have been no more than a dream. From her bed, Marta would pull back the curtains in the mornings and look out at the ravages of autumn. Only her strongest flowers were still alive – the zinnias, a gladiola spared through some unknown privilege and a few roses among those rarest kinds that dared to flower just before the frost.

She thought of summer and all she had done in her lifetime in favour of that short season, to hold it back, to embellish it, to see it flourish. How she had cherished it! As if only for the summer was it worthwhile to raise hope. Summer is a great mystery, she thought, and hope itself, and youth. Old, broken, almost dead as she was, Marta was turning back now, as if in search of herself, back to the distant regions of her own youth. She saw that her robust health and her vital energy, her love and ardour for life, had been the real part of her. Thinking of that young, almost lost being, she said, "Only then was I myself!" And she felt surprised and hurt by this, as if she had been confronted with the basic injustice inflicted on human life.

From that she came to thinking of her children. Despite the slackness of her bond with them, just to be sure they existed she would repeat their names and the names of the places where they lived.

Would it soon be time to have them come or was it too early to bother them? How would she do it anyway? If she watched out for Michael Stroulikov who came by every Thursday to pick up the cream, could she give him some message to send on? But if their father gave them a bad reception. ... Even in this extremity, Stepan was quite capable of slamming the door in their faces. Marta's thoughts wandered off in conjectures. The telephone wires took words along them. Could she not use these to speak directly to her children? She indulged in tender thoughts of them, dreaming that the wires picked them up and bore them off to Irina in Prince Albert, to Taras in Moose Jaw, to Stanley in Rorketon. For her the names of these cities where she had never been had a melancholy and captivating attraction.

Just the same, thought Stepan, this may be the time to speak to her. That would be the hardest part. The rest had been nothing by comparison. The thing was, once you'd stopped it was almost impossible to start again. Stepan brooded about it day and night. What was the right moment to speak again? For this reason or that he would always put it off a few days longer. Then, with the silence piled still higher, it came to be such a serious thing – such a concession – to break the wall at last.

How long had it lasted anyway? Two years, or three, or more than that? When was it they'd had that last quarrel over the children, after which Stepan and the old woman had almost ceased to speak? And where could he start again? At the point where language had been interrupted between them? Or anywhere at all, about the weather, for example? In the dark Stepan cleared his throat, coughed a little, tried for words that refused to come out. Was it really so hard to say, It's cold outside.... You know, old woman, I think the frost's coming this time. That'll be the end of the flowers and the garden. And the summer...but in a way, it's a relief...just the same.

That night the cold was indeed so bitter that Marta shivered under the warm eiderdown. It was one of those October nights that in a few hours devastate what is left of the patient and incomparably delicate work of summer. In the morning the sky was of that clear, unmistakable blue that presages winter.

Marta hesitated to look over toward the garden. What would she see but wilted flowers, the very death of summer? Yet she pulled the curtain back and glanced down at the little square of earth. It was her own soul she had tended there perhaps as much as her flowers. Among grasses stiff with frost she glimpsed, intact for one more day, her golden asters, mauve chrysanthemums and a few of those roses of India that reminded her of Lubka, with the consoling thought that at least Lubka had led a happy life, with her children beside her, and a good husband who had spoken to her every day.

Then, as she pulled the curtain farther back she saw close by the house a big, calloused hand lifting the little paper cones with which the plants had been capped the night before to help them resist the cold. The whole pile of Codessa newspapers must have gone that way. Now the poor old fellow would have nothing to read in the chill, lonely November days.

At the same time Stepan's grumbling voice was heard, and Marta pulled back quickly so that he wouldn't see her face at the window or feel that he was being watched.

But what she had done for her flowers at the time of their worst ordeal, the old man had done for her in return, never suspecting that he was causing the bitter cup to overflow with tenderness. But she would never be able to show it. That would frighten her old bear too badly.

That night she thought about immortality. Could it be that souls survived in some unknown region? Perhaps it was possible for certain ones: the great souls, the noble and profound minds, whose loss people would never cease to mourn. But Marta! An ignorant old woman who lagged so far behind even her own children – how could she deserve to be rescued somewhere beyond this world? No, she could not imagine herself living forever, surviving herself. Yet it was a sorrow to her, after all, that she would not continue in the spirit and sound of the wind, in the soft protest of the grasses, in the murmur of the little grove, their "grove in Poland."

The hours were running out. She had no other relief from pain than the aspirins Stepan had bought in Codessa. She doubled the dose that night, mysteriously warned that she need no longer ration her supply. Was she in great suffering? Even of this she was not sure. She would first have had to know how much others suffered, and you could have only a faint inkling of that. In any case, the aspirin helped a little. In this margin of comfort her thoughts, as if already released, rose and flew off to the past to find a distant melody. A song that spoke of summer – always summer, season of life, season of the heart – celebrating warmth and cherry trees in bloom and telling as well of young men and girls who met on a meadow to dance in the grass around a solitary tree. And through these few snatches of melody that came to her memory, these few words that floated in her mind, she felt herself mysteriously reunited with a soul unknown to her, whose nostalgic tenderness was still quite alive in this old song of the Ukraine. Was immortality then not just a dream?

What was it now that the old bearded priest had mumbled

about it when he came to bury another of them, and spoke to the handful of survivors around the earthen trench where they in turn would soon descend? It was almost always fall when there was a funeral, and the wild wind had carried off half his words of consolation. Nonetheless, Marta fancied that on those days of separation the priest had talked of space, space without end, immeasurable in distance and time. But she'd had enough of infinite majesty and space; what she wanted was mercy, what she wanted was forgetfulness. She dreamed of the prairie grasses that bend so docilely at the least breath of air.

An impetuous gust of wind passed over the little house, shaking it as if to carry it off, then was lost in the high places of the sky. She had listened so long to the wind, and with such patience, that even in this night she could tell apart all its varied elements: its sighing voice in the aspen grove; its frantic bounds over the naked plain; a short knocking summons at the window; and in the endless environs of the sky a kind of immense and despairing interrogation. Could this, after all, be eternity – that Marta herself had been wished for, and thought and decided by a Creator? All these things were too enormous for her, and too hard. Rather listen to the wind. If he remembered her sometimes, for she had loved him so much; if as he crossed the land he said something of her life – that would be enough for her: the wind in his loneliness consoling himself in her, and she in his errant spirit. . . . Suddenly voices, some of them deep, some high and shrill, burst into chorus, as if outside a city full of souls were singing in the night.

Marta crossed her hands. She sighed. To this humble immortality of air and wind and grasses she would entrust her soul.

Afterword

BY DENNIS COOLEY

All those others – Frederick Philip Grove, Martha Ostenso, Sinclair Ross, W.O. Mitchell, Margaret Laurence – wrote of the Prairies, its wind and spaces. Theirs are places where Europeans crept out, thin as thread and as brittle, into the wind, and shrivelled and died, or dried and persevered, preserved as pemmican in sun. Or they flowed in the liquid mystery of wind, in Mitchell, his prairies closest in English to those of Gabrielle Roy. Her people too come from other places, Poland, China, France, Russia, and Quebec (foreign as Europe in the eyes of her Trudeau family). They spill into the grasslands, unravel in the wind, dream of home through miles of silence, drift through "some vague zone of wind and loneliness." Baffled, they wrestle with the place, half in terror, half in love with it, as they settle into it. Blown by strange urgings to begin again, they move, at once dismayed and moved by the immensities that loom past, bloom over and under and around them.

Maria Marta Yaramko, Sam Lee Wong, the Doukhobors, the Trudeaus – strangers in a strange land – they all learn in these four closely connected stories to love the land they fear. Each finds the large troubling beauty Roy herself discovered in her prairies. Sam Lee Wong looks up to hills asleep forever and forever filled with strange light, which hang in an eternity of things you know on the edge of knowing. Horizons crush the breath out of you, sit that heavily on your chest, if you come from elsewhere, spaces fall open so vast that they swallow your songs with your spit. You yourself wallow in stillness so tall that it seems impossible to talk to or around, to get out under its shadow. An emptiness spins in the wind, in the far country, nearly erodes all language, threatens in so doing to take off what humanity you bring with you when you come to the long and distant silence.

And so you speak to it, to what you sense is there behind the wind, and you speak to yourself. You make the world your home in stories and songs, send sounds out into that numbness, even as its silence floods whole villages. The mute and secret land lies before you, able in immensity, it seems, to absorb your breath. But you breathe anyway, join the birds, breath into sound, when they bang across the dead land and cry into the frightening holes. In words and thoughts you spring free, as much as you can, from silence. There, across tracts of weeds and dust rolled on your wheels, you come across "burning air . . . filled with the presence of birds . . . creatures with flaming throats," and from the flame in your throat, from somewhere, looking for a home, you sing out into it, shake like the "great, wild birds," or Doukhobors stricken suddenly with a vision of home, shake them, with your song.

That, or you tell stories. In "A Tramp at the Door," there is Gustave, the charlatan who, hungry for the Trudeaus' fire and table, who, even as he deceives them, even as he takes advantage of their naivete, delivers them from themselves and from their land that will not yet speak to them. He speaks to their want for something more in their lives, some power and beauty that might answer to their thirst. "Gustave led us beyond all the paths we knew," the narrator tells us, and at night when the family releases him from contempt and silence, at night when there is room for stories, he takes them in and looks after them "in that spell-binding voice which sometimes sang through our house like the winds of the wide world."

This "strange creature," the narrator calls him – and so he is – comes out of the rain and the wind, brim-full of stories, ragged with hunger, restless to move, and props open windows to their lives. He is a pale-eyed figure the dog warms to, the pet badger too; he, himself creature from somewhere beyond the Trudeaus, sees into and forages in the ditches of others' lives. He gives stories that sustain and lift them, offers them, finally, the gift of story itself when the Trudeau mother, at first sceptical and resentful of Gustave, provides him with the very story he needs. When in the end she sees him off, she protects his dignity and affirms her continuity with him. In farewell she calls him "Cousin Gustave," calls him into her own story, this man hidden within dozens of names and stories.

In "Where Will You Go, Sam Lee Wong?" there is Smouillya, strange like Gustave, and child-like. He, stranger in Horizon, "had come to understand even stray cats." How fitting it is that he too should know animals and speak to the deepest knowing in those who, even as they step around him, sense his gift. True, few understand, or take the trouble to understand, when he lets fly in spittle and accent and defective speech. Yet there is almost no one he cannot understand. A bum, too, transient in others' lives, old man Smouillya, half mad for want of someone to hear him and to speak to him, listens to Sam Lee Wong, another outcast, and speaks on his behalf. And when in his elegant hand Smouillya writes the letters, speaks in fine words the unvoiced thoughts which are Sam Lee Wong's, Sam Lee would be touched with the capitals flying across the page as if they were about to take off and he would feel "a kind of continuity with certain lost things." Smouillya, another kind of conman, reads people. He seems to know what are their most cherished desires, knows how to speak to them and, if they let him, for them. He can speak, as Gustave speaks. Compassionate, he judges no one, blames nobody, an understanding ever in his words.

And then there is the anonymous narrator who, in

"Garden in the Wind," speaks of Marta, she who is herself
"a little mad and fanatical." "Who still believes in stories?" the narrator wonders. "And in any case, haven't
they all been told?" Yet the narrator does speak, released
by the rough inscription on Marta's grave – "letter after
shaky letter, as if by a hand that scarcely knew how to
write." There is a fine irony in that lettering, for it is
carved there by Marta's husband, Stepan, a man who has
become embittered by his experiences and who has
reverted to something sub-human. In *Garden in the
Wind*, that means something below speech. It is character-
istic of Roy's stories that Stepan's reduced humanity
should be measured in linguistic ways. His speech
becomes "almost indecipherable," and he himself turns
into a "savage" surrounded by "a savage silence," dropped
into his dogged speechlessness. Even as those touched
with language touch the land and its creatures, and are in
turn touched by them, they rise above wordlessness.
Marta speaks to her garden and brings it into flower,
begets a response in keeping with what she does. Others
cannot do these things. Infantile, without speech, Stepan
cannot bring the world into being, cannot create anything
in it. Those like him, wild and speechless as animals, die
in it, let the world die for want of words. For, Marta
realizes, what we do not name might fall away from us
and die out completely.

And so the heroes in *Garden in the Wind* are all namers
and tellers and singers. They talk themselves into a home,
make themselves a home, at home, even as their words are
jeopardized when the outside presses in. They "create in
this silence of God and man their little tender life, intimate and domesticated." So says the narrator of "Garden
in the Wind." So say they all, all these blue-eyed lovers of
blue, these innocents, talkers to animals and makers of
dreams. Susceptible themselves to the power of story and
to the false stories of the prairies, they can still read
inscriptions in the landscape. Everywhere they bring the
land, bring themselves, into fuller being in what they say

and hear, what they read and write. They write themselves and their people into existence, set things right with the penstrokes of roads and poles they use to ink the place.

The tellers recognize a vastness that breathes, holds its vast stillness around itself, breathing. Gustave talks of the St. Lawrence "as a living creature, a tumultuous force." Their prairie quavers with presence, shivers on the edge of speech, seems to await some call. Snow squeaks "with little, soft cries" under foot; hills undulate or sleep, or bear in fences "the tracks of an animal in a straight line across the stretch of white." At times the animals there, in the place, nuzzle people with their hot breath, will take on civilities, rise into the linguistic order, and so become human. Marta, blue Mary who sees over the plants she knows are her "creatures," and who addresses them as people, comes in a moment of illumination, in a passage reminiscent of D.H. Lawrence, to find that her flowers, even as they take on ceremonies of spirit, are palpably, erotically, human:

> Scarlet poppies with their dark core, others, their warm pink rimmed with a stronger hue, some like fine, white silk rumpled in your hand, offered their delicately pleated faces to the dry wind. . . . In double ranks lupines on their slender spikes wavered like candle flames in a wind-blown procession. But the delphiniums, now, turned back to the sky its own gaze of indifferent blue. Geraniums in brighter tones, fragile snapdragons, their small throats swollen as if from milk or honey, some flowers tall and haughty, others timid, all pressed close together as if in boundless surprise at being there.

This book is full of such passages, this garden in the wind. And think of those moments in Roy when vision falls sudden as hail from thunder or from under horses' hooves on her characters – those birds in hoodoos, the Doukhobors' hymns of loss and rejoicing in "Hoodoo Valley." There are passages where flowers stand in "bunched heads of sombre gold, purple or milky corollas with stiff, smooth leaves shining with their lacquer," where an immense land is "cold enough to freeze your breath in your throat," and "the giant sky ... dipped so low ... and lit its stars so close you could have taken them for window lights on the endless ... plain ... Could the world's loneliness at last be filled?" Lonely though the world may be, realist though these stories are, that's not all they are. In their modesty, their lyrical brevity, the simple flow of their words, their gusts of imagination, they provide a place for beauty, for grace too. They hang like a prairie mirage on the horizon of dream.

There is that poetry, then. And there is speed in these stories, a trust in summary that aligns them with fable. There are, too, the actual phrases of fable: "Yet once, having ... she ... " and "So it was that one day" and "And now a great drought ... swept down upon" and "That was how things were." Expressions like that. And there is the narrator's gentle, humane presence, so typical of Roy, her wise presiding: "Now that I think of it," "Yes," "if it really existed," "What should these poor people seek if not what lay at the bottom of that silence?" We see her willingness to forego prolonged detail and to prefer the general and symbolic. She speaks, always, in breath-taking prose, in Alan Brown's translation, which carries, carries over, into English an exquisite play of image and syntax and lively idiom. She speaks, too, in free indirect discourse, chooses to fall somewhere between the closeness (and realism) direct quotation would accord and the distance an even more indirect style would create. Stopping just short of dialogue, she writes with sympathy *and* slight dismay about certain characters. Remember those folk in Horizon who are eager to be big-hearted once they figure Same Lee Wong is leaving? Look at what the Roy narrator does by removing quotation marks and by changing the present tense and pronouns of their speech to suit her account:

The mayor stood up. He spoke for rather a long time about someone who had arrived in Horizon twenty-five years ago when the village, as they must remember, was just a few houses; and how he had worked hard with the others to make it the fine and prosperous little town it was today. A man who had laid his stone in the building and put his shoulder to the wheel! When he returned to the land of his birth, in honourable retirement from business, he could be sure that he had left behind a lasting memory.

It would take a few changes to convert this passage into quoted dialogue. And yet the words remain slightly absorbed in the narrator's account where she can insinuate a sardonic distance.

Above all, in *Garden in the Wind*, there is Roy's feel for human suffering and dignity, for the small flares of beauty and love that illuminate our lives, the moments of speech that enter the vast stillness the prairies are and seed it with life, words that blossom inexplicably on sun and wind, that stun us, suddenly, into life.

BY GABRIELLE ROY

AUTOBIOGRAPHY
La Détresse et l'enchantement
[*Enchantment and Sorrow*] (1984)

ESSAYS AND MEMORIES
Cet été qui chantait [*Enchanted Summer*] (1972)
Fragiles Lumières de la terre
[*The Fragile Lights of Earth*] (1978)
De quoi t'ennuies-tu, Eveline?
[*What Are You Lonely For, Eveline?*] (1982)

FICTION
Bonheur d'occasion [*The Tin Flute*] (1945)
La Petite Poule d'Eau
[*Where Nests the Water Hen*] (1950)
Alexandre Chenevert [*The Cashier*] (1954)
Rue Deschambault [*Street of Riches*] (1955)
La Montagne secrète [*The Hidden Mountain*] (1961)
La Route d'Altamont [*The Road Past Altamont*] (1966)
La Rivière sans repos [*Windflower*] (1970)
Un jardin au bout du monde [*Garden in the Wind*] (1975)
Ces enfants de ma vie [*Children of My Heart*] (1977)

FICTION FOR YOUNG ADULTS
Ma vache Bossie [*My Cow Bossie*] (1976)
Courte-Queue [*Cliptail*] (1979)
L'Espagnole et la Pékinoise
[*The Spanish and the Pekinese*] (1986)

LETTERS
Ma chère petite soeur: Lettres à Bernadette, 1943 – 1970
[*My Dearest Sister: Letters to Bernadette, 1943 – 1970*]
[ed. François Ricard] (1988)

New Canadian Library
The Best of Canadian Writing

Also Available in the New Canadian Library

New Canadian Library
The Best of Canadian Writing

M&S

Also Available in the New Canadian Library

New Canadian Library
The Best of Canadian Writing

Also Available in the New Canadian Library

To learn more about the author
of *Garden in the Wind*, read
Gabrielle Roy: A Life
by François Ricard

**A landmark biography that draws a
penetrating and eloquent portrait of
a remarkable literary woman.**

Despite the popularity and critical success Gabrielle Roy
found as a writer, she lived a life touched by sadness. She
was born in Manitoba, into an immigrant francophone
family marked by isolation and bitter divisions.

In 1937 she travelled to Europe to study drama and
escape the frustrations of her unhappy family life. It
was here that she began her writing career, but with the
approaching war she returned to Canada to work as a
journalist and begin, with the publication of *The Tin
Flute*, her career as one of Canada's greatest and best-
loved authors.

After Roy's death in 1983, François Ricard, Roy's
agent, assistant, and close friend, spent ten years preparing
the full, definitive account of this extraordinary woman's
life. This book is the triumphant result.

**"Few writers' lives, even the greatest, are
as exciting as the novels they write. Gabrielle
Roy is an exception – her life was the stuff of
which novels are made."**
– Remy Charest, Montreal *Gazette*

0-7710-7451-4 **$39.99 cloth**